My
Story

No Way
Back

Valerie Wilding

■SCHOLASTIC

For Elsie, who really knows B'nore
With all my love

Scholastic Children's Books
Euston House, 24 Eversholt Street,
London, NW1 1DB, UK
A division of Scholastic Ltd
London ~ New York ~ Toronto ~ Sydney ~ Auckland
Mexico City ~ New Delhi ~ Hong Kong

Published in the UK by Scholastic Ltd, 2012

Printed and bound by CPI Group (UK) Ltd, Croydon, CR0 4YY

The author and publisher are grateful for permission to make use of material from The Old Bailey Proceedings Online
www.oldbaileyonline.org

2 4 6 8 10 9 7 5 3 1

The 1st day of January, 1789

The first day of a new year, and I was in trouble before it was halfway through. I was huddled up with my little brothers and sisters, keeping warm, when Ma sent me out for bread. I grumbled, but she's used to that. She let me wear her thick shawl and I raced round to the baker's. He only had four loaves left. I picked up the cheapest, a loaf of dark bread, and held out my money.

Suddenly a kid with bare feet bumped into me, and I dropped my penny. No sooner had it hit the ground than the kid snatched it up and ran.

'Oy, you!' I shouted. 'Give it back, or I'll bash you!' And there I was, running down an alley after him, and there was the baker, running after me, because I still had the loaf.

He caught me by the sleeve. 'If this is one of your tricks, Mary Wade...' he began, but he stopped when he saw my face. I was so angry, it must have been white with rage.

'It's not a trick,' I snapped. 'Here, take your rotten bread.' I shoved it into his hands. 'That boy took my penny, and Ma wants a loaf, and now what am I going to do? She'll kill me if I come home empty-handed. How's she going to feed the kids?

And me?'

I wailed on and on, until he shook his head and walked back up the alley, pulling me behind him. I knew he would. When we got to his stall, he picked up a round loaf – quite a big one – and gave it to me.

'Here,' he said, 'have that.'

'Thanks, John Baker,' I said. I gave a great big realistic sob, although I didn't have to try too hard. I actually was upset, but I knew all along he wouldn't let us go hungry. He's a sort of cousin. We've got lots of them round our way.

I ran home, and banged the bread on the table. 'I got a big one,' I announced.

All my little brothers and sisters, except Hinny, who can't walk, rushed over to sniff it.

Ma reached across the table and squeezed the loaf. Well, she tried to.

'It's old,' she said. 'Take it back and tell John Baker he's not cheating...' She stopped, put a finger under my chin and peered at my face. 'Why have you gone all red, young Mary? What have you done now?'

I told her about the penny. 'But it doesn't matter,' I finished. 'I got bread, didn't I?'

'You got old bread!' she snapped. 'Your father will love that, won't he?'

She's not usually quick-tempered. She's worried. We've been expecting Pa for three days now. He's a drover, and he drives sheep or goats or pigs from place to place. They usually end up at the meat market, but sometimes he delivers sheep to a rich farmer, who keeps them for wool. Pa's always worn out when he comes home, and starving hungry, too. I could see that old bread wasn't much of a welcome for him.

Ma tells him not to spend his money on ale while he's travelling, but he does. He's not very clever with money, so Ma has to do all the worrying and paying. It costs a lot to feed and clothe all of us.

'Do you think he'll be home tonight, then?' I asked. I wasn't bothered for myself, because he's not always kind to me.

She turned away. 'I hope so, Mary. I don't know what we'll do if we don't get some money soon. There's only three pairs of shoes between the lot of you.' She sat on her stool and stared at the window. We've nailed up a big cloth to keep the cold out, so she couldn't see anything, except where it was torn. Her eyes shone with tears.

I picked up little Hinny for a cuddle. Four years old, and still not walking. Something's wrong there, but she's the sweetest kid. I love all the little ones. When I'm old, I'll have a dozen of my own. Six boys and six girls. Boys as tough as big Joe Smith, who can beat a horseshoe into shape faster than anyone I know. Girls as pretty and neat as the kids I see in the smart streets, all clean and shiny. I'll love them all the same, and they'll love me, like I love Ma. Only they'll be gooder than me.

When I put Hinny down, I said, 'In a way, it's lucky she can't walk, 'cause she doesn't need shoes.'

It wasn't the most sensible thing to say, so I wasn't surprised, as I turned round, to see Ma's furious face. But I definitely was surprised when she swept Hinny up and began to sob into her dusty yellow curls.

'Ma?'

'You don't understand,' she wept. 'There's never enough money.'

'But Pa's going to be home soon. He must be.' I reached down to soothe little Davey. He didn't like seeing Ma upset. Neither did I. It will be better if Pa comes home, even if he is all bad-tempered.

It was already turning dark, but I took the kids out into the yard to play, to give Ma a bit of peace. Someone always has a fire going, so it's easy to see. I found a clean patch for Hinny to sit on, and we snuggled together, all six of us, and the baby on my lap. I told them a story about a family of children called Hinny, Davey, Sarah, Lizzy-Ann, Will, Mary and baby Jem. That's us – the Wades.

In our story, which is always the same, a rich uncle comes to take us away to his great house in the country, and we ride ponies, and keep fluffy lambs that never have to go to market, and we have snow-white kittens, as many as we want. And the food we eat! Meat every meal, white bread, cherries oozing blood-red juice, and crunchy apples with no wrinkles in the skin. We have strawberries that aren't squashed and cheese with no nasty bits in it. We sleep in soft beds, and we have one bed each. A whole room each, maybe! Imagine!

When Ma called us in, we shared bowls of bread broken up into warm milk, and I helped her tuck the little ones into bed. They curled up together like bunnies in a basket.

There was a noise at the door as someone pushed it, hard. It always sticks badly in winter because of the damp.

'Pa!' I cried, but the face that peered at me through the gap wasn't my father's.

Ma wiped her hands. 'What do you want, Rowley? Where's my George?'

Rowley sometimes travels with Pa. He forced his way in and said, 'George ain't coming home yet, love. Leastways, not for a week. He's been sent off south with a new flock. He give me this for you, to be going on with.'

Ma looked down at the coins Rowley put in her hand. 'Eighteen pence,' she said. Her voice sounded flat and tired.

'He said he needs to keep the rest otherwise he won't be able to eat until he gets paid,' said Rowley. 'He'll get good money for this trip.'

I went into the other room – we've got two – to quieten Hinny. She always sleeps lightly, and the voices disturbed her.

'Good money next week won't help me this week,' said Ma. 'Good night, Rowley.'

5

'I wish I could help, love, but, you know…'

I heard her sigh. 'Yes. I know.'

When we were alone again, I went back into the kitchen. I expected to see Ma in tears again, but she wasn't. She had the look on her face that she gets when she's got something on her mind, and no one's going to interfere.

'Look after the little ones, Mary,' she said, and picked up her basket. There was something in it, covered with a cloth. 'I'll be back within the hour.'

I wonder what she had in that basket.

The 2nd day of January

I couldn't sleep last night. Even in the depths of winter, it gets hot in our bed. Hinny feels the cold badly so she always cuddles in to me. Davey likes to sleep the other way up, so I have at least one of his feet in my face. That's not nice, because he's one who has no shoes at the moment and, being a boy, he never looks where he's walking. Just as it was getting light, Lizzy-Ann fell out, so I rolled her back on to the mattress in my warm place. She squirmed with pleasure and snuggled in to Hinny's back.

I put my brown frock on over my shift, wrapped my grey

shawl round me, and went out to the pump to get water. The air was dry and still today. When I saw an apple woman wheeling her cart over the cobbles in the lane at the end of the alley, I wandered out after her. Very casually.

The cart bounced over a broken cobble, and two apples fell to the ground. As the woman bent to pick them up, quick as a flash I grabbed another off the cart and banged it against the wall.

Before I had a chance to get away, she spun round, saw me and pointed to my apple. 'You stole that off my cart,' she said. Then she turned to a couple of shoppers. 'She stole that apple off my cart!'

'I did not!' I said. 'I picked it up off the ground. It's rotten. Look!' And I held out the apple so the people could see the split skin and already-bruising fruit. That's why I bashed it on the wall as soon as I took it. 'Anyway,' I went on, talking to the shoppers. 'You don't want to buy any of her apples. She spits on 'em. I seen her.'

Leaving the woman protesting that she didn't spit on her fruit, I walked away, but not in the direction of my own home. You never knew – she might follow me, see where I live. I'm too smart for that.

Instead, I went round towards Jane Whiting's. She's my friend. A sort of friend. She's about three years older than me, but not too bright, and I suppose I look after her when we're out and about.

There was no sign of her, and I wasn't going to knock. Jane's mum isn't keen on me. She reckons I get Jane into trouble. I don't. I keep her out of it.

I wandered home, nibbling my apple. I should have eaten it straight off, because Ma had a fit when she saw me.

'You've been stealing again! What have I told you? You wait till your father gets home. He'll have you by the ears, he will...'

I tried to tell her I found the apple on the ground, but she wasn't having any of it. She never believes me. It's not fair.

'...You'll end up on the end of a rope, you will, Mary Wade.'

'You don't get hanged for stealing an apple,' I muttered, then I threw my arms round her. 'Don't be cross! At least I don't need any breakfast now.' I looked at my brothers and sisters, all chewing contentedly on what looked like soft new bread.

Ma relaxed then, and cut me a hunk off the loaf and put butter on it. 'Course you need breakfast, growing girl like you. Anyway, nobody needs to steal. We're all right now.'

'All right?' Lizzy-Ann asked, rubbing her eyes. 'What do you mean?'

'I mean,' said Ma, 'that we've got enough money. Not that it's any of your business, busy Lizzy. But we can even pay the rent.'

I wondered how on earth she got that much money, but I knew better than to ask. Anyway, I was enjoying my fresh bread and salty butter too much to talk. I did think, though.

Maybe Ma's pawned something. She had two little shoe buckles once, and she took them to Mr Wright, the pawnbroker in the Almonry, and got money for them. They give you a ticket called a duplicate, and when you've got enough money saved up, and a bit extra, called interest, you can go and get your things back. But if you can't pay it back, eventually the pawnbroker sells them. That's what happened to poor Ma's buckles. Pa wouldn't let her have any money for them.

She's got nothing left to pawn now, though. I don't think she owns anything except her clothes, and the old chest we keep all our stuff in, and her book, of course, which is her big family Bible. Ma's family were farmers, and some of them could read and write. That's why I can read and write, too. Ma taught me. Her family didn't like it when she married my pa, so they don't have anything to do with us. But her uncle gave the Bible to her just before he died and it has all the family's names written in it. He said she'd look after it properly. He used to sneak money to her, as well, so we could afford a nicer home, but that's all stopped now he's dead.

Well, she hasn't pawned the chest or it wouldn't be sitting there against the wall. Anyway, we need that to carry our stuff when we have to move on to new lodgings. That's happened a few times, when we got thrown out for not paying the rent.

So if she hasn't pawned the chest, where has she got money from?

Oh no. Not the Bible.

I waited until Ma stormed outside to tell old Biddy Barnett from across the yard to keep her stinking pig away from our door, and quickly flew over to the chest. I rummaged inside, but there was nothing hard in there except a boot with no sole that Pa's going to mend one day. It was all clothes. No Bible.

Oh, poor Ma. No wonder she was crying so hard. She must feel she's let her uncle down.

I thought I'd better check I was right before I said anything, so as soon as I'd finished helping her sweep the place out, and got all the kids dressed and looking halfway decent, I slipped away.

The wind had picked up and it was freezing. I ran to the Almonry, and stopped outside Mr Wright's pawnbroker's shop. The window was full of stuff, all with little tickets on. There were boots, a fancy mirror, a tiny, thin plain gold ring, china plates, spoons and knives, some leather straps that looked like horses' harness, and loads and loads of clothes. I saw a beautiful little blue spotted frock with white lace edging that would just about fit our Lizzy-Ann. I wish I was rich, so I could get it for her. It costs three shillings and six pence.

But there was no Bible. Perhaps it was inside.

A woman clutching a brown bonnet stepped up to the door. I followed her in. It smelled funny, sort of spicy and dusty. As she talked to Mr Wright I looked around. He was watching me, I know, to see I didn't swipe anything, so I kept my hands to myself.

And there it was! Ma's Bible lay on the shelf behind the counter. I know it's hers, because it's as big as a man's hand, and it's black. It has gold letters on it, but the top edges of the letters have rubbed away. It had a ticket tied to it, but I couldn't see the price, and I didn't have the nerve to ask, because Mr Wright's lanky assistant had appeared and was giving me filthy looks.

Before I set foot outside, I made up my mind. Somehow or other, I'm going to get that book back for my ma.

As I came out of the shop, I bumped into Jane Whiting. Really bumped! We laughed, then she looked up at the three golden balls hanging from the shop sign.

'Pawning something?' she asked.

'No,' I said, 'just having a look.'

She laughed. 'Not buying something, are you, Mary?'

'Very funny,' I said. Then I pointed to the blue spotted frock. 'See that? Wish I could get that for our Lizzy-Ann.'

'You!' said Jane. 'You'd never have that sort of money.'

I wanted to punch her. How does she know I'll never have money? How does she know I'll never live in a fine house, and have a carriage, and lots of lovely little kids of my own? She's so simpleminded she doesn't even know what day of the week it is. I hate her sometimes.

But I do need to get hold of some money, and she's pretty

good at that. You've never seen anyone look as forlorn as Jane does when she's begging. And the sad stories she comes out with! 'Oh, sir, milady, please help me! I fell off the stagecoach and my family went on without me. I have to get home! Spare a penny, please, for pity's sake!'

Huh! If I tried that, they'd tell me not to be such a liar.

'Jane,' I said, 'I need some money. Shall we go down the Treasury?'

We like going there, because there's often lots of rich people getting in and out of carriages. What you do is offer to help them down, or carry their bags, or even hold the horses' heads. If you keep on at them, they sometimes give you a halfpenny just to go away.

When we got to Whitehall, I looked to see if my friend, Billy, was sweeping the streets. When he goes off to get a drink of water, or to go to the necessary for a pee, people with clean shoes and fine clothes still want to cross the road without getting mucked up. He sometimes lets me borrow his broom while he's gone, so I can earn a few pennies. He knows I won't steal it, because I'm his sort-of cousin.

Billy wasn't there. I haven't seen him for days. I hope he's all right.

The 4th day of January

I went down Whitehall way again today, and I got a penny and two halfpennies. Billy was back, and I got one of the halfpennies while he nipped to the necessary in Treasury yard. When I've got two shillings I'll ask about the Bible. I haven't told Ma what I'm doing. I want to surprise her. It would be nice to see her happy. She's really fed up that Pa's still away. I just hope, for his sake, that he doesn't smell of ale when he comes home.

The 5th day of January

I think I've done something really stupid. I hope I'm not found out.

I looked after the kids this afternoon while Ma was out. We played outside, and I tied up some rags with a stone in the middle, so it made a really heavy ball. In my game, you had to hit someone's legs with the ball, and then it was their turn. Hinny sat, wrapped up in my shawl, while we played. It all went well until I hit one of Rowley's wife's chickens and she went mad and shooed us all into the alley. The kids thought it was great fun getting back indoors without her spotting us. Then we had a story. Hinny was allowed to choose what it was about, because she couldn't play ball. We had her favourite, about a little girl who can't walk, and a great big white bird that comes from across the sea and gives her wings. The little girl's name is Hinny, and the bird is called B'nore. She invented that. She's going to be good at stories when she's a bit older.

It was a lovely afternoon, even though it's so cold. We all had such fun. I wish every day could be like that.

Just after Ma came back, Jane Whiting turned up.

'Shall we go down the Treasury yard?' she said.

I was glad to, because I still need a lot more money for my plan. I kissed all the little ones goodbye. They hung on to me. Jane says she can't understand why I like them so much. She hasn't got any brothers or sisters. If she had, she'd know why. I love them and they love me. I don't think Jane will ever have children. She can always come and see mine, I suppose. Maybe she could live with me and my family, and help look after them.

Anyway, we went to the Treasury, and that was when it happened. Jane and I were just walking into the yard when we saw a girl carrying a stone bottle. She was much younger than me, only about seven or eight, and she was quite pretty, with shiny curls sticking out from under her cap. Her frock was deep blue, and flowery.

Seeing her in that nice frock reminded me of Lizzy-Ann, and the one in Mr Wright's window. Clothes fetch good prices. If I had a frock like that I could probably get almost enough money for Ma's Bible.

'I wish I could get that frock off her,' I said to Jane.

We followed the girl. She was heading for the pump, probably to fill her water bottle.

Jane watched her for a moment. Then she marched up and stood in her way. 'Hello,' she said. 'What's your name?'

'Mary,' said the girl.

'Same as me,' said I.

She smiled.

'And where d'you live?' Jane asked her.

'In Charles Street,' said the other Mary. 'At the shoemaker's.'

'And are you fetching water for your mother?' I asked, speaking friendly-like.

'No, for my brother,' she said.

Jane looked at me, then she tipped her head towards the necessary. I knew what she was thinking. If we could get the girl in there, we could get her frock off her. Then we could pawn it and share the money.

I smiled at the other Mary. 'Let me fill your bottle for you.'

I don't think she wanted me to, but she was only small,

and I think she didn't like to say no. I took the bottle, and filled it. Then I dropped it.

Smash!

My head was buzzing with excitement, and I truly don't know if I dropped it by accident, or on purpose.

The girl just stared at it at first, then she burst into loud wails. 'That's my mother's bottle! She'll be angry with me.'

'Shut up!' said Jane. 'I'll get you another bottle. Go with Mary and wait in the necessary. I'll bring one to you.'

'Come on,' I said. 'It's so cold. We'll be warmer there.'

Her eyes filled with tears again.

'You're not to cry,' I told her sharply.

We took an arm each and led her along the passage. There was no one in the necessary, so I led her inside. She pulled back.

'It's horrid,' she said. 'It stinks!'

'But it's warm,' I said. 'Jane will send a boy to fetch a bottle.'

That's what Jane did, and I did what I'd planned to do.

'Take your clothes off,' says I. 'It's like a game, see? We'll play the game while the boy fetches your bottle.'

'No! I don't want to.'

I wasn't giving up. 'If you don't take your clothes off, you won't get another bottle, and your mother will be angry, won't she? Come on,' I said, in the sort of voice I use when I'm playing with the little ones. 'Take them off.'

She started to. I helped her. Off came her frock and two under-petticoats. I untied her pocket, and I took her cap, and her tippet from off her shoulders.

As I piled them into my arms, she really started to howl.

Jane slipped inside. 'Shut up! The boy's coming with your bottle.'

'I don't want to have no clothes on!' wailed the other Mary.

I was worried. She was making so much noise, I thought she'd have the whole neighbourhood round, wondering who was being murdered. 'Here,' I said. 'Have your petticoats back.'

'M-my pocket,' she howled. 'It's new.'

I flung it at her. 'Come on, Jane. Let's clear off.'

We burst out of the necessary into the cold, fresh air. It was almost dark. A woman carrying a lantern and an armful of washing came down the passage towards us.

'What's that racket?' she demanded. 'What's going on?'

We didn't answer. We rushed past her, and I think I knocked the washing out of her arms. I never stopped, though.

'Come on,' I yelled over my shoulder. I'm faster than Jane. She runs with funny little stiff-legged steps, like the back legs of a donkey.

I led her to the Almonry, and we stood on the corner, getting our breath back.

'Take the frock in the pawnbroker's,' I told Jane, shoving it at her. 'Get as much as you can for it.'

She put her hands behind her back. 'I ain't taking nothing nowhere,' she said. 'You pinched it, Mary Wade. You take it.'

I glared at her. 'If I take it in Mr Wright's, you're not getting one single farthing of what I get for it,' I said.

She put on this stupid expression that really does make her look like a donkey. 'Don't care.'

I shook out the frock, and told Jane to hold the tippet and cap for me. Then I took a deep breath, stepped up to the door of Mr Wright's shop, and went inside.

'How much can I get for this?' I asked the lanky assistant.

'Where d'you get it?' He peered at me with his eyes like slits in roast chestnuts.

'It's me sister's,' I lied. 'And I'll be coming back for it soon as I can.' That was the sort of thing most people said.

He held it up. Flicked it. Poked it. 'Eighteen pence.'

'Is that all?' I whined, like the grownups always do. 'Can't you manage a bit more?'

'Take it or leave it,' he muttered.

I took it. As I walked out, I had to go past Mr Wright. He peered at me. One of his eyes is milky, and I don't think he can see very well.

I ran to Jane. 'Come on,' I said. 'Let's go round your way.' I didn't want to go home yet. I felt a bit shaky. We were lucky not to get caught, I realised. There were so many people about. If the other Mary had followed us out of the necessary, kicking up all that racket, people would have looked at her in her underpinnings and guessed what had happened.

Yes, we were dead lucky to get away with it.

Jane's mother was having a row with someone through her window, so we wandered round down New Tothill Street way to find somewhere warm and share out the money. On the corner of Perkin's Rents, where I live, I felt a hand on my shoulder.

My tummy tumbled over. I thought it must be the other Mary's father or, worse, a constable. But it was only lumpy Catherine McKillan. I don't talk to her very often. You can't trust her. She'd steal the cover off a newborn baby, she would. And the mouth on her! Never stops talking. I'd have walked away, only she's a lot bigger than me, and handy with her fists.

'Thought you two would be going down the Treasury,' she said.

Jane snorted. 'I won't be going there for a good while.'

'Me neither,' I said, without thinking. That was a mistake. It got her interested.

'Why?' she asked. 'What have you done?'

'Nothing,' me and Jane said together.

'Tell me,' said Catherine. 'I won't tell no one.' She glared at us. 'Tell me.'

We showed her the cap and tippet.

'Is that all?' Catherine scoffed. 'You won't get much for that. Hardly worth thieving, that is. You're useless, you are.'

That annoyed me. 'I got a frock an' all,' I said.

She looked at me, and I felt as if she could see right through me. 'Don't lie,' she said. 'If you got a frock, show it me.'

'I pawned it,' I said. 'I got eighteen pence.'

'If you pawned it, show me the duplicate,' said Catherine.

I realised I'd said far too much. I'm so stupid. I'm always showing off like that, and it just draws attention. 'I tore the duplicate up,' I said.

She smiled. 'Well, don't worry. I won't tell anyone. What are you going to do with the cap and tippet?'

'Dunno,' I said. I was getting a bad feeling about all this. Suppose the other Mary's mother went to the pawnbroker's shop and saw her frock there? Mr Wright might not have good eyesight, but he'd recognize me, sure enough.

'Whose clothes was it?' Catherine asked.

'A girl called Mary, lives at the shoemaker's in Charles Street,' said Jane. Donkey.

Catherine started to tell us we were silly to strip a girl and steal her clothes so close to home. 'Anybody down the Treasury might recognize you,' she said. 'You go down there so often.'

She was right. Why didn't I think of that? 'I wish we hadn't done it,' I said.

Jane snorted again. 'Well, don't look at me. It was because

of you we did it.'

I thought I'd show both of them I didn't care. 'I was in a good mind to chuck her down the necessary,' I said. 'Wish I had now.'

Catherine laughed.

I don't know if it was nerves, but I suddenly realised how cold I was. I gave Jane her ninepence, then ran up the dark alley and into our home. Even though Ma shouted at me for disappearing for so long, I was glad to be back. I cuddled Davey, for warmth. Then I wrapped my money in a bit of rag and hid it inside a hole in the wall under the window frame. Nobody will notice, because there are holes all round the frame with scraps of rag stuffed in to keep the draughts out.

It won't be long before I get that Bible back. I can't wait to see Ma's face.

The worst day of my life

Before I got up in the morning, and before the kids woke, I carefully made a little tear in the tippet. The cap is nowhere to be found. Jane must have whipped it from me in the dark. That's the last I'll see of it. Never mind that she's got legs like a donkey, she's as stubborn as one, too.

When Ma got up, I helped her get the kids sorted, and we had something to eat. Before I went out to fetch water, I put the tippet round my shoulders and waited for the explosion.

'And WHERE did you get that?' she snapped.

'Down the Treasury yard,' I said. Truth.

'You stole it! You robbed from someone's washing line!'

'I didn't.' Truth.

'Then you begged it,' she shouted. The little ones watched, with their eyes wide. 'I've told you not to beg. You'll end up in the pillory, you will, or you'll get whipped out of town, or – or...'

She's always threatening me with punishments. 'I didn't beg it,' I said. Truth. 'A woman offered it to me 'cos it was torn and she just bought her little girl a new one. Look!'

I showed her the little tear. She stared at me, and I could

see her mind working. Before she could say anything else, I flung the tippet down and said in a hurt voice, 'I can't wear it now. If I did, it would always remind me that you don't trust me.' And I ran out through the door into the falling snow, with her calling after me.

'Mary! Mary! I didn't mean...'

But I was too far away to hear.

We were all fast asleep in bed, after supper, when there was a banging at the door.

Everyone sat up.

'Pa!' cried Will and Sarah together.

'It's Pa!' said Lizzy-Ann.

'Mary, Mary, go and see,' said Hinny.

But Ma told us all to shush. She went to the door. I crawled off the mattress and peeped round to see if it was our father, back from the country. As Ma opened the door, the snow that had piled up against it collapsed inwards.

It wasn't Pa. It was the constable.

'Excuse me, Missis,' he said, and he came to stand, dripping, in the doorway of the room where we sleep. 'I want you all to get up so I can take a look at you,' he said to us children.

My poor little darlings were terrified. 'It's all right,' I said, but really I wanted to be sick. I hugged Hinny. 'She can't stand up,' I said to the constable. 'Her legs don't work right.'

'You stand up,' he said. And when I did, he said, 'You're about the right height.'

Then he looked round the room. I did, too, and when I noticed the tippet lying on our chair, I actually was sick. All over the bed, and over Sarah's foot, too.

He picked up the tippet. 'What's this, then?'

Ma reached out and took it. 'A lady gave it to her,' she said. 'That's right, isn't it, Mary? Tell him. *Tell him.*'

She looked as scared as I felt. I couldn't speak.

'You're coming with me ... Mary, is it?'

Ma pushed between us. 'For a tippet?' she cried. 'It's just a tippet. You can't take her for a tippet!'

He shook his head. 'I'm sorry for you, Missis, but it's more than a tippet. This girl is accused of taking another girl, smaller than her, into the necessary, stripping off her clothes and stealing them.' He turned and took me by the shoulder. 'Get dressed.'

And in minutes I was going out through the door, turning for one last look at my lovely little brothers and sisters, and at the face of my ma. I've never seen such an expression. It was angry. It was afraid. It was full of love.

I screamed and cried.

Once he'd taken me out of Perkin's Rents, the constable told me to stop my howling and tell him where the other girl lived.

'What other girl?' I asked.

24

He looked at me, and I must have been a sight, because my face was wet and my nose was running. I wiped it with my sleeve. I don't suppose that made it any better.

'Ow!' I said, as he squeezed my arm, hard.

'Tell me her name, or it'll be the worse for you.'

Well, who cares if I split on her? 'Jane Whiting,' I said. 'She's older than me. She wanted to put the girl down the necessary. I didn't.'

'Never mind that. Where does she live?'

I showed him. Gawd, there was a right kerfuffle when her mother opened the door. I never said a word, even when they shouted at me that I was a nasty little lying thieving – well, I won't say what else they called me – and I'd rot in hell and stuff like that.

The constable hauled us both to the watchhouse. The watchhouse keeper has a big, roaring fire, and it was so hot in there, I thought I'd die. Freezing outside, boiling inside. They wrote all about us in a book, and one of the men sitting around drinking ale told us the book would go before the Justice next morning, and so would we.

I couldn't stop shaking. The watchhouse keeper gave us a drink of water and a piece of cold meat. It was too tough to eat properly, but we chewed on it until it was time to go.

So here we are in the Bridewell prison, not far from where we live. Locked up with a load of big girls and women, all waiting to go before the Justice. Only a few hours ago, I was cuddled up with Hinny and the others. Look at me now. How long before I'm back with them again? A week? Oh no. I can't bear it.

Tuesday, about the 13th day of January

First thing, we got a bowl of broth that someone said was made with a sheep's head. I was terrified my spoon would come out with an eyeball on it, but all I found were a couple of stringy bits and a dead fly. We both needed the necessary, but there isn't a privy here, not that I could see, anyway, even though the whole place stinks like one. We had to wee in a wooden bowl thing. Then Jane and I were taken out. It was freezing and all I've got is my shawl over my old frock, and that's so thin you could spit cherry stones through it.

We went before the Justice. That other Mary was there, too, looking pleased with herself. She got to tell all that happened, and so did her mother, who wasn't even there to see it. So why they listened to her, I don't know.

Nobody felt sorry for me and Jane. She's hardly spoken since we first got locked up, so I feel like I'm completely alone. You'd think that other Mary's mother might have taken pity on a poor little child. But she didn't.

I hardly remember what was said, because it all seemed so fast, and the men used words I didn't understand. But in the end the Justice explained what's going to happen to us.

It's terrible! We're being sent up the Old Bailey tomorrow, to the Sessions House. That's the court where criminals go, to be tried. I'm frightened. Two of the old women here said we'll be put in Newgate prison, and locked up for ever and ever. They can't do that, can they? Not just for taking a stupid girl's frock and stuff?

One of the younger women, who wears a very grand gown, though it's shabby, said we mustn't worry. 'They wouldn't do that to little girls,' she said. I smiled at her, because she was kind, but Jane went in floods of tears. She's tall for her age and isn't a little girl at all. I'm going to try to look very small when I go before the judge.

I want my ma. I even want my pa.

Wednesday, about the 14th day of January

They took us on a cart. They put us on a big, rattling cart with some other prisoners, and they drove us all the way through the city to the Old Bailey. The snow was deep and the horse kept stopping and straining. Steam was rising off its coat, but we were all so cold. Jane and I huddled together. We were shaking. Partly it was cold, but partly it was because we were so scared.

Little kids pointed at us and laughed and called us names. One pretended to put a rope round his neck and dangled his head with his tongue lolling out, as if he was hanging. I've done that to prisoners on carts. I'll never do it again, I swear.

When we reached the street called Old Bailey, a bald man in the cart pointed to the huge building next to the Sessions House. 'Newgate,' he whispered. 'That's where we'll all end up. And we won't never get out.'

I started to sob. Jane was already crying so much her hair was sodden.

A woman slapped the bald man's arm. 'You shut your mouth,' she said, and she put her own arm round my shoulders. 'She's just a little 'un. They won't be hard on her. What d'yer do, sweet?' she asked me, lifting my chin up.

'Took a frock,' I said. 'Pawned it. Took a tippet, too. And a cap.'

'Oh dear,' she said. 'You'd better look at the judge all blue-eyed, then, hadn't you? Else you'll be in for it.'

I sobbed even more at that. My eyes are brown.

My trial

Inside the court, it was huge. And cold. All the doors and windows were open, and I could see snowflakes flying past. It seemed so crowded, and most of the people were dressed properly. No rags or dirty clothes. Their shoes were clean and shiny, and their faces looked like they'd been polished. Lots of the men wore wigs, so I suppose they were law people.

And the room! The ceiling was so high you'd have to be a bird to reach it. There were benches of shiny polished wood, and brass rails. I never saw anything like that, and now I know I never will again.

What happened was this: me and Jane were stood in a sort of wooden box, so everyone could see us. There was a lot of talk I couldn't understand, and banging of a hammer to shut people up, and then the judge spoke. He was called the Lord Chief Baron, and he looked very stern. He seemed cross before he started, and his face was bright red underneath his big white wig.

I didn't understand what was going on, and then I heard a man call a name out loud and clearly. 'Mary Phillips!'

It turned out she was the other Mary, and her frock and cap and tippet belonged to her pa, who was called John Forward.

A lawyer man stood up and cleared his throat with a lot of noise, then he asked Mary Phillips how old she was.

'Eight years old,' she said.

Then he asked her if she knew what she was there for – about her frock – and if she would tell the truth.

'Yes,' she said, in this little whiny voice.

But when the man asked if she knew the difference between what's the truth and what's false, the stupid thing said, 'No.' So she was sent off, and her mother, Jane Forward, was what they call sworn in. That means they swear on the Bible to tell the truth. That choked me a bit, because it reminded me of Ma's Bible.

One of that family is a liar, because the mother said her Mary will be eight next April.

When the lawyer asked Mrs Forward what happened on the evening in question, she said that her girl met her at the door, crying, 'Mother, I have been robbed.'

Then after Mary's brother had said his bit about sending her for water, Jane and I had a dreadful shock. The next person called was that witch, Catherine McKillan!

I couldn't believe one of our own kind was going to tell on us, but tell on us she did. All about how we met by Perkin's Rents, and how we told her what we'd done. She said I told Jane I wished I hadn't done it, and how Jane said it was my own fault. Then she added, 'The little one said, "I was in a good mind to have chucked the child down the necessary, and I wish I had done it."'

That got everyone in the court tutting and mumbling things like, 'Shocking!' and 'Disgraceful!'

As if that wasn't bad enough, it turns out it was Catherine who went to the shoemaker's in Charles Street where the other Mary lives, and told her mother who had stolen her stuff.

My ma and pa will skin Catherine McKillan alive when they hear about this.

Next was the woman with the washing who I'd bumped into. She'd gone in the necessary when she heard the other Mary howling, and she looked after her. She said that a girl ran past her very quick, but she never said it was definitely me.

The other person who couldn't say it was me for sure, was the pawnbroker's assistant with the eyes like slits. He got muddled up between me and Jane when he was asked who took the frock in. He said he reckoned it was the tall one – Jane – who brought it in, but that it was my name that was signed. I was glad he said it was Jane. I thought the judge might think Jane had forged my signature, then he could put her in prison and let me go.

After that they called Constable Taylor, the man who arrested us. He said he first heard about the whole thing when Catherine and the other Mary went to tell him. I hate that Catherine. When Mr Taylor told his story, he said, 'The little prisoner told me that the big one wanted her to put the child down the necessary.'

I was pleased about that.

The judge spoke to Mary Phillips again, and he was quite fierce with her. He told her that if she didn't tell the truth, she'd be punished, and she went all tearful and said she would. I looked at her and her curls and her clean clothes, and I knew everyone would believe her. No one would believe anything I said – that's if I got a chance – when I looked so dirty. I pulled my fingers through my hair and tried not to scratch.

Mary Phillips blamed everything on me more than on Jane. She even said she knew me – that she'd seen me sweeping the streets.

I could see it was all going badly, and I almost stopped listening. My heart was thumping and Jane was sniffing beside me, when I suddenly heard my own name. I looked up. The judge was asking me how old I am. I told him I'm going on eleven. Then he said, 'Have you no friends?'

Well, I've got loads, so I said, 'Yes.'

'Are they not here?' he asked.

If I hadn't been so frightened, I would have laughed in his face. My friends! Set foot in a place like the court! I told him they came but they weren't allowed in.

And that was it! He never asked me anything else at all.

He spoke to Jane and she said she was going on fourteen.

Then my heart almost stopped. My ma walked up to where you had to stand to speak to the judge. She looked small, and so tired, and her face was the colour of dough before it's cooked. She looked at me and I felt she wanted to put her arms round me, but of course, she couldn't. I just mouthed, 'Ma,' without making a sound. They'd warned us not to speak unless we were spoken to.

Ma said she was my mother, and how old I was, and about my pa. Then that horrible judge told her she was as much to blame as me, because she didn't take proper care of me. I'd like to have pulled his yellow teeth out for saying that. My ma loves us all and she feeds us and cares for us, even when my pa doesn't.

He didn't stop there. He said she should keep me busy. I'm always busy! I never sit still for five minutes, except with the little ones.

'You are at fault,' he said to Ma, 'for letting her run about the streets.'

'It's the other girl that induces her out when my back is turned, to go a-begging with her,' said Ma. 'I never brought her up to go a-begging.'

When the judge heard how many brothers and sisters I have, he told Ma, 'I hope you will take better care of the rest, or else they will all come to the gallows.'

The gallows! That gave me a shiver, but I put it out of my mind, because I was having trouble understanding what the judge was saying to the jury people. He went on and on, and I only took in odd words, what with Jane snivelling next to me, and Ma sobbing into her sleeve.

He droned on, and I noticed even some of the jury people looking a bit fidgety. I heard the words 'actual robbery' and 'dangerous', and then a voice called out, 'Guilty!' and the judge put a piece of black material on his head.

Then I heard one more word. It was 'Death'.

Everything happened so fast. Ma screamed and stretched her arms towards me, but two men held her back. Jane was a crumpled heap on the floor until she was pulled to her feet, and then we were bustled out of the court and everything was a hideous blur.

In Newgate prison

I can't remember what day it is. It might be Friday. Or Thursday. It doesn't matter. Only one thing fills my mind and it's black. Like cold, dark night.

I have been sentenced to death. I am to be hanged by the neck until I am dead, and they hope God will have mercy on my soul.

Jane was sentenced to death, too. She spoke not a word after that, but neither did I. Next thing, we were being hurried through a dark passageway that seemed to be under the ground. There was a metal grid in the ceiling at one point and I remember it dripping water on to my cap as I passed beneath.

There were questions, and inspections and washing. I can't remember much of either, except for my hair being pulled about as someone poked through it, searching for lice and fleas, I suppose. Finally, we were thrust into a cell. There must have been fifty women in there, but hardly any of them so much as looked at us at first.

I found a space against a wall and sat down. The floor was cold and damp. Jane curled up and lay in my arms. I held her like I would hold Hinny when she hurt herself, but I so desperately wanted someone to put their arms around me. I wanted Ma to hug me and make this horror go away.

But Ma's not here. Maybe she can come to see me. But there might not be time. I don't know how long it will be before they hang me.

After a bit, a woman with hard, cold eyes came to talk to us. She smiled, but her eyes stayed cold. She asked if we had money. When I said we hadn't, she said, 'Best tell the truth, girl. If you got money, it'll get pinched. You'd best give it to me to look after for yer.' I managed to convince her I had nothing, and she went away, only to be followed by another, and another. They mostly said the same thing, until a very thin girl, not much older than Jane, crept over and sat down beside me.

'I haven't got anything,' I said, 'so don't ask.'

She reached into her bodice and pulled out a piece of dark bread. 'I thought you might be hungry,' she said.

It was the first time anyone had been kind to me since the constable came. I couldn't speak. All the tears I'd been holding back came flooding out. She stroked my hair with her bony hand as I cried.

When I couldn't cry any more, she held out the bread. 'Eat it. You must eat, for your strength. Go on, I don't want it.'

I broke the bread in half and tucked Jane's piece inside my dress. She'd fallen into an exhausted sleep. Then I ate. The bread was dry and it was hard to get it down, but I did.

'I'm Sal,' said the girl. 'What are you in for?'

I told her.

'Are you being transported?' she asked.

I must have looked stupid.

'Transported,' she said again. 'You know, sentenced to be taken on a ship across the sea to a wild land on the other side of the world. Is that what they said will happen to you?'

I shook my head.

Sal frowned. 'You're not? What's your sentence, then?'

'D-death.' I started sobbing again.

Sal called to two older women, and told them about me and Jane. One of them, called Elizabeth Barnsley, said, 'Don't you worry none, ducks. They don't hang little girls.'

I looked up in hope. 'Don't they?'

She looked uncomfortable. 'I'm sure they don't.' Then she turned and shouted to the rest of the prisoners in the cell. 'Here, you lot. These nippers have been sentenced to the drop. Treat 'em right. They're only young, especially the little'un.'

Some of the women looked sympathetic, but others just turned away, like they didn't care. A few didn't even appear to have noticed Mrs Barnsley speaking. They just stared into space, looking hopeless.

Lizzie Barnsley seems to be important. No one messes with her, and if she says do something, it gets done. She's got money so she pays two shillings and sixpence a week to sleep in a separate room, with sloping boards to lie on, so you're not on the damp floor.

Sal found Jane and me a place to sleep next to her. I was glad she was so close. It made for a bit of warmth. I didn't sleep all night. There's so much noise. Cries. Screams. Shouts of anger. And soft whimpering, the sounds a child makes when it's been sent to bed with a few slaps and no supper.

The floor is hard. There is some straw, but most of it has been snatched up by prisoners, so they can use it to lie on, to try to soften the hard floor. What's left is sodden and it stinks, for there is no privy here, just a thing like a pail, in the corner. It soon gets full. Some of the women have just given up trying to keep nice. They lie in their own filth on the floor. Everywhere stinks so badly, but Sal says I won't notice it after I've been here a while.

If Mrs Barnsley was lying, then we might not be here long enough to get used to the noise and the stink.

The beginning of February

Jane has become one of the prisoners who just sit and stare all day. She won't even get up when we're allowed to go outside, unless I make her, which I do.

I love being outside, but sometimes I wish we weren't allowed out at all, because it makes it so much worse coming back in to the dark and the stink. I think it must smell really badly in the yard, too, because when you see visitors walk through, they have handkerchiefs pressed to their noses.

Sometimes, if prisoners bother a visitor, he will throw a handful of coins into the air so they will dive for the coins and leave him to make his way through. There's such a dreadful scramble for them. I never bother. What could I get from the turnkey with a halfpenny? A piece of cheese? A candle? The cheese would be snatched from me by one of the big, heavy prisoners and, after the candle had burned, I would still be in the dark. One big girl had a candle brought in, but she had no means of lighting it. Another prisoner offered to get it lit for her. Of course, the poor girl never managed to lay a hand on it again.

The only thing that brightens my life is a visit from Ma.

But when she is gone, I feel worse than ever, and don't speak to anyone for hours. She brings me food, and watches me eat it. I always keep some for Jane, whose mother is rarely able to come all this way. Her legs are not good. Ma also tries hard to make sure I have something clean to wear. I notice that her own clothes are becoming more and more patched and mended. One day she brought me an extra shawl, and when I asked where hers was, she said she'd left it at home, as it was a mild day. After she'd gone, two things happened: it began to snow, and a woman from another cell snatched my shawl and threatened to punch my lights out if I ever mentioned it again.

Pa never comes. Ma doesn't mention him. Is he so ashamed of me that he doesn't want to know me any more? I talked to Jane about it.

'Perhaps he never came home,' she said.

She might as well have kicked me in the stomach. I can't bear to think of Ma looking after all the little ones on her own, and with a wicked daughter waiting to be hanged.

A Saturday in February

We're still here. Jane has perked up, because everyone keeps telling her they don't hang little girls. She's not as little as me, but she isn't grown up, so she says she'll tell them she's really a little girl. I think she's a bit daft.

I know it's Saturday, because that's the day we get a piece of beef, as well as the usual hunk of bread. The meat's horrible, all fat and gristle. It's tough, so you have to chew it a lot. That's good, really, because it lasts such a long time.

My scalp is all scabby, because I scratch it so much. The bugs in here drive me mad. I hate creepy-crawlies, but you can hardly see an inch of floor that's bug-free. As I walk, I can hear lice crunching under my shoes. There's an old woman in here who keeps shouting about how it's cruel to kill living creatures. I don't care about bugs. If lice are dead, they won't be eating at my scalp. Fleas, now, that's another thing. You have to be very quick to catch a flea. They hop. I tread on anything I see moving.

My shoes themselves are falling to bits. I never take them off. If I did, they'd be gone in two minutes. The place is full of thieves, and none of them care if they're seen stealing something. If they are, there's a big fight, and everyone gathers round, egging them on, and whoever wins the fight gets the goods. I can't risk anything of mine being pinched, because I'd lose a fight in about two seconds. Jane's got hardly anything left, just the clothes she stands up in. I've still got my old shawl, because when I don't wear it, which is hardly ever, I stuff it down my front.

Sunday, a week later

Apart from Saturdays, you can't tell the days apart here. Except for Sundays. We always know when it's Sunday, because the church bells ring out. When they do, I close my eyes and picture myself in the fresh air, with the smell of wood fires, and the rustling sound of ladies' skirts as they hurry to church.

Then I open my eyes to this grey world that stinks like a hundred necessaries on a sweltering hot day when the city is crowded. And I'm cold, and my feet are damp, because it's been raining and the water trickles in through every crack in the walls it can find.

Sal is so ill now that she can hardly move. And still she won't eat. One woman, who calls herself Emerald, has been kind to her. She makes Sal suck on a piece of cloth dipped in the water they give us to drink and wash in. I reckon that's what's keeping her alive. Mrs Barnsley says there's nothing to be done for her. She's determined to starve herself to death rather than be transported across the sea to a wild country where she'll be killed and eaten.

This wild country they talk about is on the other side of

the world. It's called New South Wales, and some ships went out a year or so ago to start what they call a colony. From what Mrs Barnsley says, it sounds ghastly. There's no houses or shops.

'So what do you do when you need food?' I asked her.

'You grow it,' she said.

Stupid woman. I'd like to have said, 'Show me a bread tree, then. Show me a pie plant.' But I didn't. You don't get cheeky with Mrs Barnsley. She's been here nearly a year, Emerald reckons, waiting to be transported, and she says she's not scared.

Elizabeth Barnsley is not the sort of person to be scared. People are scared of her. Well, maybe not scared, but they're very wary. She sort of rules this place. But she can be kind. I just wouldn't want to get on the wrong side of her. I've seen what happens to people who do.

One day when we were outside, it was so cold, Jane and I didn't want to walk around, and she showed me how to play a game called noughts and crosses. You have to draw lines in the dirt with your finger, then you take turns to put a nought or a cross in a space, and if you get three in a row, you're the winner.

I always win.

But today I didn't. The weather was bitter, but we weren't going to give up our precious time outside the cell, so we huddled down on the ground and played over and over.

There was nothing else to do. We'd had about twenty games. Jane never got cross about losing. She pretended she let me win because I was younger than her. I don't care. I know the truth. Anyway, I was dimly aware of two women talking nearby – one a lot older than the other, who didn't look as if she had the wits to commit a crime. What they said went like this:

'Shall we go inside?'

'I dunno.'

'D'you want to?'

'I dunno. If you want to, we can. D'you want to?'

'I dunno. I can't decide. What do you think?'

'I dunno. I can't decide, either.'

It got on my nerves so much that I looked up and snapped, 'Why don't you ask Mrs Barnsley to decide? She decides everything else.'

I was aware of Jane's gasp beside me, and the two women staring open-mouthed at me. The next thing I knew was a great thump in my back that sent me sprawling in the dirt.

Then from behind came a voice I recognized.

'I've decided that you're a brat, and you don't deserve my kindness.'

I looked round into the tight-lipped face of Mrs Barnsley. It wasn't her who'd thumped me. It was one of her cronies – the gang of women who hang round her, hoping for little presents.

46

Mrs Barnsley reached down and pulled my arm, dragging me upright. Then she stooped, put her face so close to mine I could smell her beery breath, and hissed.

'So I decide everything, do I? Well, you should thank the stars that up till now you've had a friend in Elizabeth Barnsley, because if it wasn't for me, you'd be half dead by now. These women –' she gestured round the yard, '–would have had every stitch off your backs within two days of you being here, and you'd be rat fodder by now. And that food your mother brings you? You eat it, don't you?'

I nodded.

'You only eat it because I allow you to! It's never stolen because I've given orders that you're not to be treated badly. Think on that!'

And she flung me back down, spat on the ground, and walked away into the silent yard.

I cursed myself. I'd made an enemy of the most important person in Newgate, as far as I was concerned. Even more important than the turnkey.

I got shakily to my feet, and turned to Jane for comfort. I didn't get it.

'I won that game,' she said. 'You didn't see, 'cos you fell on top of it, but I won.'

Liar.

I always win.

The middle of February

It's so cold in here. I can barely feel my feet. One of the turnkeys slipped on an icy patch in the passage to the Sessions House and his leg's broken. Everyone laughed and jeered when they heard the news. I didn't. He's the only one who's not completely cruel. He doesn't push people to the floor when he brings them in. Most of the others do. He lets them walk in on their own feet.

Water leaks in everywhere. My shoes are nearly in shreds, so my feet are always damp. Freezing cold, too. It's only going to get worse when the snow thaws. Water running down the walls and across the floor. It's impossible to keep the straw dry. I keep imagining our cosy, crowded bed at home.

Tuesday, the 24th day of February

Ma visited today. That's how I know it's Tuesday. She brought me a new shawl, thicker than the one that was stolen. It's brown, and what she calls coarse.

'But it'll keep you warm,' she said, and gave me some fresh bread – light, almost white bread. She said she didn't have to pay for it.

'John Baker sent it for you,' she told me. 'And here's some good cheese and a bit of boiled bacon. I would have brought you fruit, but there isn't anything – nothing I could afford, anyway.'

I tore off a piece of bread with my teeth. 'Thank John Baker for me,' I mumbled. And as I gulped it down, I remembered the day I was buying a loaf from him and I dropped the penny. That kid – the one who picked it up and ran off with it – was it because of him that I'm here? Or is it all my fault?

Ma's never mentioned the Bible. And neither have I. She just held my hand in the yard today, with white streaks down her face where the tears had run. She said she's got a cold, that's why she's all bunged up, but I know that's not true. She must have cried all the way here.

As I chewed the cold bacon, she told me all about the little ones. Baby Jem has got a new tooth, and Davey broke one of his when he slipped on some of old Biddy Barnett's pig mess and fell over a step. Hinny is as sweet as ever, she said, and they all miss me and send me kisses.

Ma never actually gave me those kisses, but I could imagine them all the same.

She didn't say much more. I know that when she goes, she wonders if she'll ever see me again. I can't bear to think of that.

I knew she'd be going home soon. She's always hated being round strange streets and alleys at night. I wrapped the leftover bread and the cheese in the new shawl. When it began to grow dark, she said she had to go and put my brothers and sisters to bed. That made me cry, imagining bedtime. I'll never sleep in a bed again.

As we walked across the yard, there was a sudden commotion in a corner. One of the women had caught a rat, and two others were fighting her for it. A live rat's worth an extra hunk of bread. There's a man in one of the other cells who's made a little cage out of pieces of wood. They say he puts a rat in the cage, then feeds it, and when it's fattened up, he lights a fire with wood his friends bring him, and cooks the rat. He pays the finder the bread on the day he eats the rat. That's why the women were fighting over it.

When Ma had gone, I went to see what was happening.

There was a fair old argument, and Mrs Barnsley was right in the thick of it, laying down the law. When she saw me, I quickly dodged behind Jane. I didn't want to attract her attention.

Once we were locked up in our cell again, Jane and I tried to find a dry place to settle down for the night. I whispered to her that I had something tasty to share with her. She leaned forward and kissed my cheek.

'Mary, you're so good,' she said. 'I think I'd be dead without you.'

She's got big weeping sores on her mouth.

Another squabble broke out, and I got to my knees to see what was going on. One woman snatched something from another and fought her way across the cell. She bumped into me and sent me sprawling. I swore at her – that's one thing I've learned how to do in here – and got to my feet.

And when I looked down, my food had gone. And my new shawl. Stolen. In an instant.

I knelt down in all the filth and I sobbed and sobbed. Ma had walked all that way, and heaven knows what the little ones had had to go without so I could have that food.

Jane hugged me all the while. After a bit I was quiet, and just flopped against her. Suddenly she pulled away from me. I looked up.

Elizabeth Barnsley.

'That's taught yer, ain't it?' she said. 'Don't cheek yer elders. I was good to you and you threw it right back in my face.'

'I'm sorry, Mrs Barnsley,' I said.

'Then it's a good lesson learned,' she said, and held her hand out to the side. One of her cronies, a woman called Maggie, put something into it, and Mrs Barnsley held it out to me. 'Your cheese. Half of it, anyway. Right tasty, that was, wasn't it, ladies?'

She looked round at her grinning friends. 'I couldn't stop them, you see. They like a bit of cheese, they do.'

I took it from her. 'Thank you, Mrs Barnsley,' I whispered.

'And here's yer shawl,' she said, flinging it to me. 'I can't see you freeze, kid like you, all skin and bones.'

Maggie tittered. 'If you can call that a shawl, eh, Lizzie? I wouldn't be seen dead in it!'

Another woman snorted. 'No.' She stabbed a finger at me. 'But she might be.'

Mrs Barnsley froze them with a look. 'You shut your faces. She's just a kid. She has to learn to live in here with all you thieving witches, but we don't mock her for what's going to happen to her. Right?'

A wave of dizziness washed over me, and I managed to get to the wall before I was violently sick. Then I cried. All that good food I'd eaten, wasted.

The 25th day of February

I was so glad of Jane's warmth last night. At least I wasn't alone. There are prisoners in here who never speak to a living soul; they just huddle against the walls scraping at the wet green mould with their ragged fingernails. Many are to be transported across the sea. There's Rachel, who lies next to us at night, who's got to go for seven years. She'll be allowed to come back after that, except everyone says you can never save enough money to get back to England.

But what I want to know is this. Rachel stole some clothes, a bit like I did, *and* she stole some money. So that's worse than what I did. So how come she wasn't sentenced to death and I was? That isn't fair. She says it's the luck of the judge. Jane and I had a harsh one. Rachel's been kind to me, and keeps telling me to stay chirpy. 'They'll never hang a little girl like you,' she says.

Early March

There was an execution this morning, so it must be Monday. You could hear the crowds shouting and jeering, and then a deathly hush, and then that horrible moaning, wailing sound at the moment the prisoners are hanged. Jane and I looked at each other. We've been at a hanging often enough, seeing what we can get hold of. People don't watch their pockets when they're being pushed and shoved in a crowd. If I ever get out of this place alive, I'll never go to an execution again. And I'll make sure my little brothers and sisters don't ever see one, either. Or my own kid, if I ever have them.

What am I thinking! All I ever wanted was to grow up and marry someone with some money, and have lots of dear little children. That'll never happen now. I'll never be a mother.

March

The weather must have warmed up a little bit. I can feel my feet when I wake in the night now. Feel the fleas nipping them, too. I suppose spring's coming, though you could never tell in here.

I keep on the right side of Mrs Barnsley now. If she wants anything done, I try to nip over to her before any of her cronies do. People have all sorts of different names for the cronies who suck up to her all the time: toadies, spongers, crawlers, leeches. Jane said I'm turning into one, but I'm not. I'm just being smart – I keep on the right side of her. Ma used to talk about Horrible Sukey, down our alley; she used to say, 'Best to keep on the right side of Horrible Sukey. You might not want her as your friend, but you certainly don't want her as your enemy.' That's how I feel about Mrs Barnsley. Rachel says she's not as bad as you think, but I'm not too sure. Rachel seems to see the good in most people, and in my opinion, there isn't always good to be found.

The 15th day of March

There was practically a party in here today. A woman called Barbara who came in last week has spent practically every waking minute shouting and bawling about how she's innocent, and they were going to put her to death for something she hasn't done. Even Mrs Barnsley couldn't shut her up.

Well, she won't be executed! She heard today that her sentence has been changed. She's going to be transported instead, for fourteen years. It seems they caught the man who actually did the murder, and he confessed. But she's not happy about it.

As they brought her back to the cell this afternoon after telling her the news, we heard her shouting, 'You can't send me to be eaten by savages! I'm innocent! Innocent! I never murdered no one!'

I whispered to Rachel, 'They can't send her across the seas, can they? Not if she's innocent?'

Old Dinah, who's been in here longer than anybody, heard me. She cackled and said, 'Innocent, my back teeth!' (She hasn't got any.) 'It must have been her what put the bloke up to it. She'd have been pardoned, else, wouldn't she?'

A sudden cheer went up. Mrs Barnsley had given the turnkey money for some booze – ale or wine or something – and she said everyone could have a swig. Bet she used to like a party when she was free.

I didn't want any, and nor did Rachel. Jane went to try it and came back making such a face that I couldn't help laughing. I laughed and I laughed, and I kept on laughing, louder and louder and then louder still. I laughed and laughed. Then suddenly, tears were rolling down my cheeks. Was I laughing or crying? A bit of both, I reckon.

Rachel stroked my head until I calmed down. A word was ringing through my brain. Pardoned.

I went over to where Mrs Barnsley and her friends sat, enjoying their booze. I touched the shoulder of Nelly with the red nose, who's one of her cronies. 'Do people get pardoned?' I asked.

She looked up at me. 'Eh?'

'Pardoned. Do people get pardoned? Let off? Set free?'

Nelly Rednose grinned, showing four grey teeth. 'Yes, little Mary. We had one in for murder just afore you arrived, that got pardoned and sent outside,' she said. 'They found someone who saw what happened, and they said she didn't do it. She was innocent.' She laughed nastily. 'But you're not innocent, are you?'

I swallowed. My silly hope that I might be pardoned, too, was blown to ashes. I turned away, but jumped when I heard

Mrs Barnsley's harsh voice. I turned. Her face was stuck right in front of Nelly's.

'Shut up!' she snapped.

'I warn't doing nothing,' Nelly said, defiantly.

'You was trying to frighten that poor kid.'

'I warn't.'

Mrs Barnsley reached out and shoved Nelly Rednose in the shoulder. 'Don't you argufy with me,' she barked. 'Keep your mouth shut.' Then she turned to me. 'Don't take no notice of her,' she said, gruffly.

'Thank you, Mrs Barnsley,' I whispered. I bit my lip.

'If they was going to hang you,' she said, 'it would have happened by now.'

I do hope she's right. Even if they make me stay in Newgate for ever, at least there's a chance I'd be able to see my brothers and sisters again, one day. Oh, how my heart aches for them.

Next day

It's strange. When Jane and I were locked up in here, I imagined we'd spend our last days alive being close friends and comforting each other. But that's not what happened. Of course, we stuck together at first, and we still – well mostly – huddle together to sleep. But now Jane sits and walks with the older girls. I don't have any friends apart from her, and poor Sal. But Rachel is good to me, too, and lots of the women talk to me, and some of them are quite nice, like Eleanor, who's here for forging a will. She was kind to me when I was upset, and now I'm being kind to her because she's feeling poorly.

There are two new babies in here, and I sometimes hold them for their mums, to give their arms a rest. You can't lay a baby down in this place. It would be trodden on, and get bitten by bugs, or even rats.

And it's nice having a little cuddle. I miss that.

The 19th day of March, very cold

There's talk that King George is cured of his madness and has been getting better this last couple of weeks. I didn't even know he was mad. Why do we have a mad king? Surely it would be better to have one that wasn't off his head.

One new prisoner, once she'd got over the shock of being in Newgate, said that people have been celebrating the king's recovery in all the taverns. I expect my pa did, too. Any excuse for ale, Ma always says.

There's going to be a proper right royal celebration, she says, when the king's completely better. I won't see that right royal celebration, that's for sure. Maybe my brothers and sisters will. But someone else will have to carry Hinny.

What does a girl like me have to do with a king, anyway? He's not going to pardon me, is he? Not if he's busy with parties and things.

Three days later

Jane and I have been here so many weeks – I don't know how many – that I'm starting to believe, to hope, that I won't be executed. But if I'm not, and if there's no pardon, does that mean I'll have to stay in here until I die? If I do, I don't think it would be long. Mrs Barnsley was right when she said I was skin and bone. I've got a cough, too. Ma says it's the damp, and promised to make a warm onion poultice for my chest. It will be cold by the time she gets here.

I can't see Sal today. Not surprising. She's just skin and bone, too – worse than me – and when she curls up on the floor she just looks like a little pile of rags.

Everywhere is sodden. It's rained all day, and the water runs down the walls and across the floor. There's nowhere dry.

Later

Poor Sal has died. It's made me cry.

The 1st day of April

The turnkey shouted down through the passages this morning, 'By order of His Gracious Majesty, what is getting better, all prisoners are to get a flask of wine and a roasted fowl for dinner today.'

Well, how we drooled and dreamed. All morning we talked of the treat in store, and the older women blessed the king, and some of us could even smell the whiff of cooking on the air.

We should have known better. When dinner arrived, it was nothing more nor less than water and bread.

The turnkeys laughed and laughed. 'Don't you know what day it is?' said the chief one. 'I'll give you a clue. You're all fools. Geddit? All Fools!'

That's how I know it's April the 1st.

Mid-April

There's a rumour going round. If it's true, it frightens me. Some of us girls and women are to go back to the Sessions House in the Old Bailey, for a special hearing. The last one was bad enough. I don't ever want to go there again. I can't stop shaking.

Next day

Oh, I do want to go to the Old Bailey again. I do! At least, I think I do. They're saying that King George is going to pardon some of the women who are down for hanging. Well, maybe not pardon, but he's going to stop them being executed. Oh, will I be one of them? Jane hugged me when she heard. She hasn't even bothered to speak to me lately, so ordinarily I'd have told her where to go, but I'm so mixed up, I was glad to have someone to hug me.

Later

I've just had a dreadful thought. Could this be another cruel joke being played on us by the turnkeys? Oh, I couldn't bear it. My heart is high one moment, and low the next. I feel sick, and I cannot think straight.

The 23rd day of April, St George's Day

Bells have been ringing through the city on and off all day, and one of the visitors said people were having a special holiday. It's the right royal celebration because King George is better.

But I can't think of that. Tomorrow on Friday the 24th day of April (I've been in here for three months!) I'm to go back to the Old Bailey. Jane's going, and Eleanor, the forger, has got to go, too, though she begged not to, because she's unwell.

Later

I can scarcely believe what's happening. They say we're going to be given a reprieve. A reprieve! It's a sort of pardon, but not a proper pardon. It means they're going to offer a change to our sentences. Those of us who are sentenced to death will be offered to change it to being transported to the land called New South Wales. If it's true that it's on the other side of the world, it must be an awfully long way away.

Oh, I'm in turmoil. If this is true, it means I will live! At least for a while longer. Who knows what will happen across the seas? The women tell dreadful stories of people being eaten, not just by wild animals, but by men!

But I mustn't think of the worst. The women who have been sentenced to transportation, like Mrs Barnsley and Rachel, have either got seven or fourteen years. That seems like forever, but it isn't, really. If our sentences are changed to transportation, Jane and I might get back to England one day. No, not 'might'. Will.

Maybe I'll see my little brothers and sisters again! Maybe one day I will have kids of my own. Oh, it's like the sun's come out, even in this dark, stinking hole.

Please, please, let it be true.

The 24th day of April, the day that changed my life

Oh, what a mess my mind is in! What a jumble. I feel woolly in the head, my heart feels light, yet I am scared.

Names were called this morning, and mine was one of them. So was Jane's. The turnkeys made us have a proper wash – well, our faces and hands, anyway, and then we were led along that gloomy underground passage, which I know now is called Dead Man's Walk, back into the Sessions House. Last time I was there all hope was snatched from me.

This time, I walked in full of hope. Some of the women with me are murderers. I never did anything bad like that. Surely, I kept thinking, surely they'll give me a chance to live, even if it is in a wild land.

We went into the court and were lined up together while the judge read out all this stuff in words I didn't understand. But I did understand the words 'His Majesty' and 'pardon' and my heart leapt, because then I knew it was really true. I am not to die!

Next, we were each asked if we accepted the pardon, and would agree to transportation to 'parts across the seas'. That means this New South Wales place.

'Yes.'

'Yes.'

'Yes.'

And so it went on, until it was my turn. 'Yes!' I said. 'Yes!'

But to my surprise, suddenly I heard, 'No.' And then again, 'No.' And once more, 'No.' I looked to see who was speaking. It was a serious-faced woman called Martha, and Eleanor, who's not well, and Sarah Cowden, who has always sworn she's innocent.

Altogether seven women said no. I can't believe they did that. Imprisonment in Newgate, maybe death, in exchange for a sort of freedom in the fresh air and sunshine, for New South Wales is said to have good weather?

We, the ones who said yes, were taken back to our cell. The others stayed. Will we ever see them again?

Mrs Barnsley got a whole tray of pies sent in by a gentleman friend, and the ones she and her cronies couldn't eat, she let us share; by 'us', I mean the ones who'll be going to New South Wales alongside of her.

I'm still very careful with Mrs Barnsley, though, to be fair, she's not been unkind to me lately.

Next day

After feeling so happy, both Jane and I can't stop crying. Mrs Barnsley says when you've had a lot of worry or excitement or a shock, and then something good happens, often you do feel bad afterwards. That was kind of her to say so, but it hasn't made me feel any better. What's really breaking my heart is that I haven't got seven years, or fourteen years. I've got life! That means I can never return to England, no matter how much money I save up.

The women who said no to transportation were sent back here to have a think, and everyone's bullying them to make them change their minds. They say they won't.

The end of April

Mrs Barnsley has gone! She has been taken to the ship that will sail with her to New South Wales. It's much better now, because I don't worry all the time that she'll get angry with me.

The 1st day of May

It's May Day, someone said. I don't know why it's so cold. Maybe it's warmer outside these stone walls.

Newgate's not really better without Mrs Barnsley. She used to keep a certain gang of women in order, and now each one of them is trying to take her place. There's constant fighting and screeching. I keep right out of the way.

Rachel has gone now, too. I wonder if she will be on the same ship as Mrs Barnsley. I miss her. Several others have gone, too – all women for transportation, so still no one has been executed.

It's ages since we've seen the women who said no. The turnkey told us they've been put in cells all on their own, and they're getting just enough to eat and drink to stop them dying. 'That'll change their wickedness, ungrateful trollops,' he crowed.

People have been telling us about New South Wales, and about the fleet of ships that went there a couple of years ago to start the colony. It's not a proper town. It's huts and tents, I think. There are no markets, no cook shops, no churches and NO PRISONS. At least, I don't think so.

The 3rd day of May

The weather must have changed. It's so hot and stuffy today. The only thing that's cool is the floor, because it's always damp.

I made a mistake about there being no prisons in New South Wales. The whole colony-thing is one big prison, except there are no fences or walls to keep people in. That's because no one in their right mind would run away. There's nowhere safe to go. There are poisonous snakes, and spiders that can kill a grown man! There's a big animal that hops, and it has great long legs and feet that can kick you. Bears live in the trees! Just imagine if you were walking along and a great bear fell on top of you! And there are huge dangerous fish in the sea, called sharks, that can eat a whole man. They sound as if they are as big and fierce as dogs.

I don't like the sound of it. But anything's better than the hangman's noose. Ma cries every time she visits, which isn't so often now. She's having another baby and the journey is getting too much for her. She says Pa is hardly ever at home. All the little ones send me hugs and kisses, especially poor little Hinny. Ma says she cries often, and misses me dreadfully, because the others haven't got the patience to help her get around.

All the women who said no to transportation have said yes, and are back with us. They look terrible – thin and weak, with dark rings beneath their eyes. But some of them still have their spirit. Sarah said, 'We'll soon be fat and healthy now we're back with you. Amazing what a few days of good food and fresh air will do!' Everyone laughed at the thought of us having good food and fresh air!

Good food! I've forgotten what it was like. If it wasn't for the bits Ma brings me, I think I might be dead.

The 6th day of May

Oh lawks-a-mercy, we are to go out of here tomorrow to join the ship we will be sailing on to New South Wales. I have seen ships on the river, and they do not look safe. It would be easy to fall off into the water. The top bit, where the sailors walk and do their work with the masts and sails, is called the deck, and everyone says there are rooms below deck, where we will live. Perhaps it will be safer there.

Ma hasn't been this week. If she doesn't come today I may never see her again. But she never comes on a Wednesday, and that's what today is. There's something I want to ask her. I want to ask it so badly.

Later

It's almost dark. Ma didn't come. Now I can never ask her if she managed to get her family Bible back from the pawnbroker. He will keep it a long while, but not for ever.

I will never sleep tonight. Jane is snoring, and Eleanor, who is to come with us, is crying quietly into her sleeve. I can't cry. I don't think I've got any tears left. I will surely never see my little ones again.

The 10th day of May

We are on board a ship called *Lady Juliana*. It's a huge ship. I should say, 'She is a huge ship,' because everyone calls ships 'she'. There are no sails, because we are still in the river, but I can see them rolled up, ready to be unfurled.

That first morning, the day we left Newgate, Jane and I were woken in the dark, along with the other women who'd been to the Old Bailey with us. We were allowed to wash our hands and faces again, and then we had irons put on our wrists. A few of us had our irons chained together. They were loose enough so you could scratch your nose if you needed to, but we couldn't run away. If we did, we'd have to drag the others with us. I did think about it. And so did Jane. Her eyes darted everywhere as we were led out of the prison to some waiting carts.

Dawn was breaking, fires were being lit and the air smelled good. So fresh and sweet. A flower seller was setting out her roses and lilac. After the drab grey of Newgate, the vivid colours of the flowers almost sparkled. As we rumbled through the streets, we saw market people getting their baskets and stalls ready. That was when I got a shock. Those market women, who had always seemed so ordinary to me, suddenly appeared smart and shiny clean. I looked at Jane and the others, at their hair, hanging in limp dusty rat-tails, at their grimy faces, and their ragged clothes. Did I look like that? I knew I did, and I was ashamed.

It was even worse when passers-by called out things like 'Phwoar!' and 'Stinking hags.' In prison, the stink was from the slime and slurry on the floor, from the necessary buckets, not from us. Or so I'd thought. Now I knew we stank as bad as any corner of Newgate.

At Blackfriars, we had to get into a long boat. The guards

took off the chain that linked us together so we could get in safely. I dare say they knew none of us would be so stupid as to jump into the water and try to escape – not with our wrists in irons. It was scary. I've never been on a boat before, and I didn't realise how much they rock. I thought how much worse it would be on the big ship.

As the boat was rowed swiftly away from the shore, I worried that we might crash into another one. The river is so busy. I've seen it hundreds of times, of course, but I never took any notice of what was going on. We travelled past warehouses, barges being loaded, then as the river grew even wider, we passed places where men worked on ships: mending them, loading them, cleaning them. I suppose if you go to sea in a ship, you need to look after it, otherwise it will sink.

Soon we came to a row of big boats that appeared as if they'd never been looked after. They were rusted and rotting. One of the guards pointed to the worst one; its masts were broken off and the stumps looked like giant splinters against the early morning sky. Rotting ropes, rusted chains and filthy rags hung from its sides. 'There's yer ship, eh, ladies,' he said, then burst out laughing at the look of horror on our faces. 'You're all right,' he said. 'Your ship ain't like this. She's seaworthy – won't get to New South Wales else.'

He told us the rotting ships are called hulks. They're ancient ships that are no good for going to sea. They still have a use, though. They've been turned into floating gaols. Prisoners eat and sleep on them, and during the day they're taken ashore, chained together, to work – if they're fit enough.

We rounded a slight bend in the river, and there, before us, was the ship that's going to be our home for months and months – the *Lady Juliana*.

'It looks all right,' I whispered to Jane. She nodded, but continued staring upwards as we neared it. The deck was very high. How were we to get there?

The seamen had it all organized. Ladders made of rope were let down, and we climbed up and over the side on to the deck, which is made of long planks of wood, scrubbed clean as clean. Everywhere is spotless. It looked beautiful after our prison cell.

Then everything happened in a whirl. A kindly-looking man with soft brown eyes hammered the irons until they broke away from our wrists. We were taken down some steep steps into what the sailors call 'below', and stripped of our clothes by some of the women prisoners who were already on board. They weren't unkind, but they didn't waste time. We washed thoroughly. That felt good, except for being watched by strangers. Then we put on a clean shift, which was a wonderful feeling, some brown convict clothes and a plain white cap. When they saw my shredded shoes, they gave me some more.

One of the women cried when her dress was taken away, but she was hushed by the prisoner who handed out the clean things.

'You must be thankful there's such a kind and good agent to care for us,' she said. 'It's the rule that your own clothes must be taken away, but he's given orders that they may be kept for us. He says we'll need them when we get to New South Wales, and they'll remind us of when we lived in England.'

There were quite a few sobs as she said this, and I realised Jane and I aren't the only ones whose hearts are being torn apart at being taken so far from our families. It had never occurred to me that all the prisoners must be leaving behind someone they love.

We live down below in a big space called the orlop hold. It's near the bottom of the ship and it stinks. Somewhere nearby is a place called the bilge, and it's where all the rubbish of the ship ends up. It smells like dead rats and rotting cabbage and pig muck when you go below, but after a while, you don't really notice it quite so much. When we're taken up on deck, though, the clean air smells wonderful.

Behind a wooden wall at each end of our hold are two more holds. These carry all the ship's stores. It's funny to think that we've been without enough to eat for so long, and now there are heaps of food so close to us!

We sleep side by side on wide ledges. It's like lying on a

shelf. There are no windows, of course. A little light comes through the gratings in the roof of our hold. But how much better, how much warmer, how much cleaner it all is than Newgate prison.

Everything would be altogether better, if not for one thing. Mrs Barnsley is here. I truly thought she had gone on some other ship, but no, she is here, and as loud as ever. She makes me feel uncomfortable, because I have annoyed her in the past. And I know how easy it is to cross her. I am afraid of her tongue. Rachel is here, too, but that's good.

Mid-May

The kind man with the brown eyes is called Mr John Nicol, and he is the steward of the ship. He is very friendly with Sarah Whitlam, one of the younger women, who has been aboard for many weeks. He has told her that when we are at sea, we will be allowed on the deck. I wonder if we will be allowed to walk around freely, or if we will be chained or, at least, tied to the ship in some way.

Sarah says Mr Nicol is as kindly as he looks. When he goes ashore, if a prisoner asks him, and if she has the money, he will fetch little things for her. He doesn't treat the prisoners as if they are dirt on the bottom of his shoe, as the turnkeys in Newgate did.

I said, if Mr Nicol is our gaoler, then we are lucky. But Sarah said no. The man who is our gaoler is called the agent. His name is Lieutenant Edgar, and he is responsible for delivering us safely to New South Wales. I remember that the man who is storing our clothes for us is the agent. Lieutenant Edgar cannot be too bad a gaoler then, if he does good things like that.

Mid-June

A whole month has gone by and still we live in the hold. We are allowed visitors on board before we leave, but no one has come to see me. I feel so alone.

Late June

Ma came to see me at last. She has been too ill to go out, but as soon as she was able, she went to Newgate. When she heard I wasn't there, she felt her heart was breaking. She thought I had been hanged, until she found out what had happened to me. She had to beg lifts on carts, and walk, and spent two full days getting here. It was late afternoon when she arrived, and she was exhausted. I have reason to bless Mr John Nicol. He took pity on her and sent a seaman to fetch food and drink for her. Not only that, he gave her a handful of pennies, enough to buy her space in a lodging house for the night. 'So you will be fresher for your long journey tomorrow,' he told her. Ma took his hands and kissed them, and said she hadn't been shown such great kindness from a stranger ever in her life before.

'Look after my Mary,' she begged him. 'I've nothing to give her, for her father has deserted us and I have a big family to feed.' She laid a hand on her belly. 'And more to come.'

Mr Nicol swore I would have food aplenty, and that I would not be alone. Then, under his watchful eye, I was allowed to walk with Ma to the ladder of rope. I clung to her, and we both wept. Mr Nicol came to ease my grip on her and held my shoulders as I watched my mother being rowed away. The last I saw of her was her silhouette and her waving hand as she disappeared into the grey evening gloom. She will never visit me again. It is much too far, and the ship might sail any day.

A seaman was standing by to escort me back down into the hold, but I was crying so much I could barely walk. Then a hand took my arm, and the quiet voice of Mr Nicol said, 'I'll take her.'

He walked with me, and through my tears I saw Sarah Whitlam come towards us. Mr Nicol is right friendly with her. She is about ten years older than me, and she calls him John.

'How did a little lass like this come to be here?' he asked Sarah.

She didn't know, and I found myself telling them everything. About the penny, and the Bible and what I did, and how I didn't really mean Mary Phillips harm, how I just wanted money to get Ma's Bible back.

'And does he still have the Bible, this ... what's his name? Mr Wright? The pawnbroker?' asked Mr Nicol.

How would I know? 'Probably,' I said.

He told Sarah to be kind to me. She held my hand, and patted it. She is a much nicer person when she's with Mr Nicol, I think, than when she is with the rest of the women.

Once I was back in the hold, I curled up alone on my bedding. It is very thin, and it smells musty, but how wonderful it is to have it, after the slimy, stinking floor of our Newgate cell. Everyone is happier already, though sad, too. Even Mrs Barnsley is not as frightening as she was in gaol. She is wearing drab brown clothes like the rest of us, but boasts that she is to be allowed her own fine clothes when we are at sea. Dull and coarse as my convict dress is, it's far better – and cleaner – than my own dress, which has become just rags.

The end of June

Two more days have passed and something has happened which I can scarcely believe. No one has ever done such a kindness for me before, no, never in my whole life.

A seaman looked down the ladder to the hold and called out, 'Mary Wade! Is Mary Wade there?'

I didn't answer. My heart had suddenly screwed up like a crumpled kerchief. There could only be one reason for me being singled out. My time had come. They had decided to execute me after all.

I slid behind Rachel, whimpering. 'Don't give me away. Please,' I begged.

'Mary Wade,' came the voice. 'Don't keep Mr Nicol waiting.'

Still I didn't move. Not until I heard Mr Nicol's own voice say, 'Mary, come up on to the deck. Don't be afraid.'

I trust him. I don't know why. I've never trusted any man before. I crawled out from behind Rachel and squinted up to the light.

'That's her, innit?' said the seaman. 'Come on up, little 'un.'

I went to the ladder. Behind him I could see Mr Nicol's

face. There was no sternness in it. I climbed up and he reached out to offer a hand. Then he led me to the back of the ship, behind a chicken coop, and sat me on a long wooden chest.

'I have a gift for you,' he said.

I stared at him. I had never had a gift in my life. 'What do you mean?' I asked.

He reached into the large leather pouch he always carries with him, and took out something wrapped in a cloth. 'Here.'

I took the package and peeled open the cloth. What I saw brought a great sob to my throat. It was the Bible. My mother's Bible. I stroked the black leather, and ran my fingers over the faded gold lettering.

I could not speak, not even to thank Mr Nicol.

He seemed to understand. 'You can return it to your mother now,' he said. 'Will that make your fate easier to bear?'

I nodded. I could scarcely see his kind face, because my eyes were so full of tears. He asked where my family lives, and said he would send the Bible himself.

Before he took it from me, I kissed it.

My last day in England

We are to sail in the morning, on the tide, whatever that means. A man called Captain Aitken is in charge, and it is his decision.

Later

Terrible. It's terrible! I can't stop crying.

Earlier today, a seaman called Sarah Whitlam up on deck. When he brought her back, she took me by the hand.

'Come,' she said, and she wouldn't tell me what for. She led me up on deck, where the seaman was waiting. He led us through a small doorway and down a short steep ladder. Then he knocked on a door, opened it and told me to go in. Sarah waited outside. I stepped over the threshold into a tiny room, which I now know is called a cabin. There was a narrow bed on one side, like a long box with no lid, and in a chair by a small polished wood table sat Mr Nicol. He looked very serious, and reached out a hand to me.

'I'm sorry, little Mary,' he said, and it was then that I saw what lay on the table.

It was Ma's Bible.

He read my expression. 'No, no, I did try to send it. The messenger had to bring it back, because your family have moved. A neighbour said your mother was unable to pay her rent, and moved on.'

I nodded. It had happened before.

He lifted the Bible and placed it gently in my hands.

Sarah took me back to the hold.

Early July

We are at sea! I never in my life thought to see so much water! You could put the whole of London on the sea and still there would be more all around! On one side I can see the land, far away, but on the other it is all water, water, water. And how it churns! The little waves at the edge of the River Thames are nothing! The sea rolls ever onwards towards the land, and the waves burst and tumble in little storms of bubbling white foam.

The sea has a smell, too. The river smelled, of course, but

this is different. It is a green smell, though the sea itself is grey. The seamen say it is sometimes blue, sometimes even turquoise, which is a colour I don't think I have ever seen. I like the smell.

We are allowed on deck for much of the time now we are at sea, but we've been ordered to keep out of the way of all the seamen, who dash about with ropes and hooks and chains. They must know what they're doing, but it all looks a jumble to me. They shout a lot, too – not in a bad-tempered way, but telling each other what to do, or what they have just done.

The sails fill with the wind, and it's that that moves the ship along. When I peer over the side, the water rushes by, so we must be going fast, but when I look at the land, it's as if we're hardly moving at all. We are going to a place called Portsmouth. More prisoners will come aboard there. Aboard! I'm already sounding like a sailor!

Sarah says Mr Nicol told her that when we start to travel south, it will get hotter, hotter than the hottest summer day I can imagine. I don't believe her. How can it get hotter than summer?

My Bible is wrapped in its cloth, inside my bedding. It is hard to lie on, but if I can feel it, I know it's safe. I don't think anyone will take it. Most of the women who saw it laughed, especially when they saw how much it means to me.

'What good's a book going to be when you meet the savages in New South Wales?' one asked.

Another said, 'Maybe she could read a story to the lions in the jungle – if she could read.'

I didn't let on that I know how to read already. They wouldn't believe me, anyway.

I told Jane they made me sick, laughing at me. She said I should tell them I kept the Bible because it's worth money, so it'll come in handy when we reach New South Wales. Then they won't think me stupid.

'It's not worth anything to anyone else,' I said.

'Mr Wright, the pawnbroker, thought it was,' she said. 'You'll be able to sell it, maybe.'

'I would never sell it,' I said.

'I would,' said Jane. 'If it was mine, of course,' she added quickly.

I glanced at her and thought, I'm watching you, Jane Whiting.

A few days later

We've dropped anchor near the town of Portsmouth. From the sea, it looks a bit like London, only much smaller. We can see little else, as there is a sea mist which mixes with the smoke from the town's chimneys. There are prison hulks here, too, and dozens of little boats being rowed back and forth.

We were all sent back down below. I suppose that's in case we decide to jump off the ship. That would be stupid. Even in the mist we couldn't help but be seen. If we didn't drown, we would be clapped straight back into prison.

More prisoners came down the wooden ladder into our hold, and I was shocked to see how filthy they are. Did we really look like that? Sarah says we looked worse, because we were from Newgate, which is the worst prison in the world.

There's a ship here called *Guardian*, she told me. It – I mean 'she' – is going to follow on behind us, and it will be loaded with stores. We will not be welcome in New South Wales, John Nicol told Sarah, if we don't bring food and seeds and animals and things. The people already there have barely enough for themselves. There are awful tales about them all being sick and starving. We'll have to supply our own shelter and our own beds. Everything, in fact, except water. There's lots of water there.

Mid-July

As we left Portsmouth today, we were at last allowed on the main deck again. The mist has thickened. After just a short while, Jane wandered over to the left side of the deck – the sailors call it the port side, which seems odd, as I was on what they call the starboard side, and I could still see the port of Portsmouth.

Suddenly, Jane screamed. 'Mary! We are there! I can see New South Wales!'

Two sailors nearby roared with laughter. 'You've a mite more distance to go yet, little lady,' said one.

The other told her (I pretended to think it as funny as they did) that what she could see was just a big island. 'The sea is all around it, like it's all around our own land,' he said.

I had not realised that I lived on an island. I suppose it was because I had never seen the sea.

The end of July

We are in a very busy port today, called Plymouth, in the county of Devon. Before we were sent below, I saw boats of all kinds, many with big cannons. We are having water brought aboard, and if there is a quiet moment – which there isn't often down in our sleeping hold – I can hear barrels being rolled along.

More prisoners have come aboard, too. One young girl, not a lot older than me, just kept muttering, 'Stupid, stupid, stupid!' all the time. An old woman, who had been in gaol with her, said that the girl was in a tiny prison near her home, and was let out to help with harvesting something or other. Every hand was needed, they said. She had to promise to go back to the prison, so she did. Now she wishes she'd run away, and all she says is, 'Stupid!' I agree with her. I'd have run.

Sarah let me help her tidy Mr Nicol's cabin, and she told me he's gone ashore to get more cows for us to take, and more chickens, and some fresh vegetables. I swear I have heard a pig. In past days, as I wandered the streets, if anyone had told me there was a pig on one of the boats in the river, I would have punched them for being a liar.

The 29th day of July

Today was a shock. Not because of what happened, but because of how it upset me.

We were allowed up on deck as we started to sail south, then Jane and Sarah and I listened to the seamen as they got ready to sail west past a sticking-out bit of land called a headland.

One of the older seamen, who is always happy, though he swears a lot, rubbed the top of my head. 'Look your last on England,' he said.

It was then that I felt as if I had been kicked in the tummy. I think that ever since we left London I must have been putting my sadness in an empty place in my head. Now I suddenly had to face the truth.

Unless there is a miracle, I will never see Ma, or Pa, or Hinny, or Lizzy-Ann or any of my little darlings ever again. And the children will grow up and forget me.

Oh, I can hardly bear it.

I went to the rail and looked out to sea. I felt it would break my heart to watch England disappear. When I finally turned round, there was no land in sight. I spun round in a panic. There was no land anywhere. We were completely surrounded by water. We still are.

Early August

Every morning I climb up to the deck and look around. It is still the same. Just sea everywhere. Birds fly over the ship sometimes. I wonder where they land.

Jane doesn't like my friendship with Sarah. Even though we sleep side by side, she scarcely speaks to me. She's taken up with a group of girls of about eighteen or nineteen years old who are loud and who swear and sometimes fight.

Many of the women squabble and fight. It frightens me. Some of them have killed. Who knows? They might do it again. I know there are men to guard us and keep us safe, but a murder takes just a moment, Sarah says.

I must try to make everyone like me, even Mrs Barnsley. Then I will keep out of the way of trouble. I shall help people. I shall make myself useful, and they will all grow fond of me.

Mid-August

Mrs Barnsley has had a change of heart. She has plenty of money and possessions for herself, and is being quite kind to the poor women and girls, like me, who have nothing. In return, she does like to have them do her bidding. She hardly has to do a thing for herself. There's always someone ready to mend her skirt, or fetch her a drink.

Sarah reckons Mrs Barnsley wants to make sure she'll be looked after when she gets to New South Wales. The rest of us will have to take care of ourselves, but she's making sure she will always have people to look out for her. She's promising all sorts of favours when we get ashore. I wish that could be soon.

The weather has turned nasty, and some of the women feel sick. One of Mrs Barnsley's new band of cronies, who I call Mean Moll, was sick over the side of the ship this afternoon. The wind blew it right back in her face. I did laugh.

Next day

Today the weather was bad and the wind whipped the sea up. It was frightening to watch and Captain Aitken ordered us down below. It was for our safety, and to get us out of the way of the seamen, who were flying about all over the place with ropes and tools.

We do try to keep our orlop hold as clean as possible, and fresh air is let in from above all day. But we can do nothing about the stink from the bilge. Today that was soon made even worse, because the ship was being thrown about so much that many of us were sick. I wasn't, I'm glad to say, but my face must have looked green. Sarah was nowhere to be seen, and I found out afterwards that she was safe in John Nicol's cabin. She told me she is expecting a baby and it will be born on the journey, so Mr Nicol is taking care of her. Those of us who could move around without throwing up did our best to help the sick ones. There wasn't a lot we could do except clean them off and wipe their foreheads.

Tonight the sea is calm.

The 17th day of August

Sometimes, when I help Sarah clean John Nicol's cabin, I see what date he has written in his journal.

Most of the women and big girls have work to do, like scrubbing and sweeping, and cleaning out chickens and milking cows. I haven't got a job. Lieutenant Edgar said I'm to make myself useful where I can.

When we left Mr Nicol's cabin today, the cook was sitting on deck in the sunshine, peeling apples. I offered to help him, and he looked at me with his one twinkling eye. 'Can I trust a wicked young convict like yersel' wi' a knife?' he asked.

I protested that I was not dangerous and he laughed, and said he was only teasing. I sat beside him on a box and peeled away. The smell of the apples made my mouth water. He said I could eat some peel strips if I liked, so I was sneaky and cut my peel more thickly, so there was more apple to scrape off with my teeth. I saved a few pieces for Sarah, but she turned up her nose at them and said John gives her all she craves to eat. John is Mr Nicol.

It would be sensible of me to keep close friends with

Sarah. I shall offer to brush her hair. She is very vain about her hair. I can't see anything special in it myself.

The 20th day of August

Everyone is very tired and crotchety. For two nights we have been kept awake by a woman called Martha. She is having a baby, and it will surely come soon, for she is huge. But each night she started wailing and crying out, saying, 'It's coming! Oh, it's coming!' I'm sure we all wish it would, just to shut her up, but Mrs Barnsley says it won't be today. She knows all about these things and has already delivered one baby since we left England. Sadly it died almost the moment it was born. The mother cried a lot, but Mrs Barnsley says it's all for the best. What sort of a start in life would it be for a baby, born in a stinking hold in a ship that never stops moving, and taken to a land of fierce animals and jungle and man-eating wild men and fish with teeth?

The 21st day of August

The baby has at last been born. It came in the early evening, and we were all allowed to stay up on deck if we wished while Mrs Barnsley was delivering it. She asked for helpers, and though I wanted to get in her good books, I kept well out of the way. Seeing a baby born is not new to me, for I helped Ma once, but I had no wish to listen to the mother crying out so loudly. Anyway, the weather is beautifully warm now, even in the evening, so it was good to lie in a sheltered corner of the deck and look up at the night sky.

I saw a shooting star and tried to make a wish before it disappeared, but my mind was so full of jumbled wishes that I couldn't put one into words. What a waste.

The 24th day of August

The baby is a boy and is named George, after the king. I would not name my baby after a mad person. But little

96

George is sweet and I sometimes hold him when his mother takes a few steps around the deck to build her strength. I do love babies. I miss my own darlings. Do they think of me, I wonder? Does Hinny miss me? Does someone else help her to get around?

Next day

Such a funny thing! Since we left Plymouth, a woman called Nance has caused trouble again and again. And every time she's been punished by being put down in the hold with the hatch on. It's very hot, and no one can bear to be down there unless they have to. So most of us thought she was just stupid.

But – and I know this is true, because Sarah told me – Mr Nicol was checking some stores in the hold next to our orlop hold, and he found a large cask that should have been full of bottles of strong beer. The bottles were there all right, but the beer was missing.

The thief turned out to be none other than Nance! She had made a hole in the dividing wooden wall, crawled through and drunk her fill!

Her punishment was horrible, but so funny. She was put

in a barrel herself. Her head was through a hole in the top, and her arms through holes at the sides. Nance didn't care! She danced and pranced about the deck, making everyone laugh. But when she grew tired, it was a different matter, because she discovered that she couldn't possibly sit down!

Lieutenant Edgar refused to allow her out until she apologized to him. She did, and she promised to be good in future. We shall see.

The 27th day of August

Nance has been in trouble again, and she got a dreadful punishment, far worse than the barrel. She was behaving so wildly that she was given twelve strokes on her back with a special whip called the cat-o'-nine-tails. It has nine separate strands, each with a knotted end. She's quieter now.

The 30th day of August

We reached an island yesterday, called Tenerife. Its port has a foreign-sounding name too. It is called Santa Cruz. 'Santa' means 'saint' in the language they speak here.

Now the ship is no longer sailing, it feels so hot. It's hotter than the hottest summer day I've ever known. In London, on a day such as this, everywhere would stink, but here there is a breeze, which must blow all the bad smells away.

There is a town on shore, and behind it I can see mountains, and there is snow on the top of them! How can it be so hot here, and be cold enough for snow there?

The 1st day of September

While we are in port, we can have all the water we want, and there's been a great deal of clothes-washing going on. We have had fires on deck to heat huge pots of water and have hung our clothes to dry wherever there is a space. One of the sailors said they wouldn't need sails if we would just leave all our fal-lals, as he calls our bits and pieces, hanging around.

The 4th day of September

Mrs Barnsley gave everyone a treat yesterday. She handed some money to Lieutenant Edgar and he allowed a whole cask of wine aboard for her. I truly thought she might have wanted to drink it all herself, but she didn't. She shared a good deal of it, and anyone who wanted any (apart from four or five women who she will have nothing to do with) was given some. Even Jane Whiting had some. She doesn't seem to mind the bad taste any more. I tasted it, but could not bear it. And when I saw what it did to the women who drank a lot of it, I'm glad I didn't have any. They tottered around with stupid grins on their faces and then collapsed in snoring heaps on the deck. Two of them had to be kicked awake, so they could go below for the night.

Mid-September

All the water and food Captain Aitken wanted is on board, so we have set off again. Our next port is called São Tiago. It seems that 'São' also means 'saint', which is very confusing. I hadn't realised there was more than one foreign language. At home I either understood people, which meant they were speaking English, or I didn't, which meant they were speaking foreign.

I wondered aloud what language they will speak in New South Wales. Sarah laughed at me, but I noticed she didn't tell me, until she'd seen Mr Nicol, that they speak English there. That's a relief.

Late September

It is still September. I caught a glimpse of the date in the book that Mr Nicol writes in, but could only see the month. Sarah does little work in his cabin now, as she is huge in the

101

front. The baby will not be born for two months, she says.

After about a week of horrible, hot weather, we have left São Tiago. I am glad. I have never been so uncomfortable, except in Newgate. When we were locked up below, it was unbearable. Everybody just lay around, sweating and moaning. The babies (we have three now) cried and added to the stink.

October

It was such a funny day today! We're at the middle of the earth or something, and there's a line called the equator which we had to cross. I never saw it, though I leaned overboard for a long time looking for it. I felt so stupid when one of the seamen told me it's an imaginary line. But I think they must be stupid, too. Why pretend to cross a line that isn't there? It's like me sitting on deck saying, 'I'm just going to eat this mutton chop, when my hands are empty!'

But crossing this equator is the excuse for some frolics! When we were finally allowed on deck it was to see the strangest sight. At first I thought I was looking at half man and half fish. But it was one of the seamen, with a mop upon his head, and a crown, and he was called Neptune, who is the king of the sea. The reason he was half fish is because the sailors had caught a gigantic fish – a porpoise – and they'd emptied out its skin, and Neptune's legs were inside it. The seamen said Neptune is a merman. He had a wife, too, who was a very old sailor dressed up. His face was as wrinkled as an apple that's been kept all winter.

There was a lot of water-throwing and singing and all sorts of merry-making, but I didn't understand most of it. The sailors drank, and the captain joined in a bit. It wasn't long before most of the crew and a lot of the women were dozing in odd corners of the deck.

As it grew dark, I found a nice sheltered spot where I could hear the chickens cackling and the pigs grunting, and I lay and watched the stars until I fell asleep.

It was a nice day.

Mid-October

We are heading for a port called Rio de Janeiro. I wonder if 'Rio' means 'saint', too, but I'm not risking Sarah laughing at me again, so I shan't ask. She is quite bad-tempered these days. She is hot and finds it difficult to get comfortable. She will be glad when the baby is born. How lucky she will be to have a baby of her own.

We are to be at Rio de Janeiro for several weeks. This is bad news, because it means we'll be locked up whenever there are other boats near, just in case we try to escape.

Next day

We're barely moving at all at the moment, because the wind has dropped. It's so still and quiet. The heat below is unbearable, so most people try to find a sheltered spot on deck. But there is no breeze to cool us. I feel sorry for Sarah in this heat. She says she would love to rip her clothes off and throw herself into the sea. She would surely be eaten if she did. The one-eyed cook has told me tales of giant creatures. The octopus with eight arms! And sharks, and squid, and fish that look like jelly rather than fish, with long stinging strands trailing from them. Some of those stings can kill a man, so I don't think Sarah would last long.

Late October

I have taken care to keep my belongings safe. I don't have much, and of course my Bible is my precious thing, so I keep it well hidden inside my bedding. But today I found my shawl was gone. I don't need it because I am as hot as the inside of a baker's oven, but I would like to know where it is, and which thief took it. Now I worry about my Bible every time I leave my bed. I'd be really upset if that disappeared or if it was damaged in any way. I feel I owe it to Ma to take care of it – for as long as I can, anyway.

The 2nd day of November

Rio de Janeiro is much too hot for me. I wonder if New South Wales will be like this. Today there wasn't even a sea breeze to cool us. We have loaded up with coffee and sugar. All day long, we heard the rumble of barrels as they were rolled along the deck and into the hold where the provisions are stored. Now we are anchored well off shore, and we are likely to be here for some weeks.

There is a mountain here, called Sugar Loaf Mountain. I have never seen a sugar loaf so I don't know what it is like. To me, the mountain looks like a great giant's tooth sticking up out of the earth.

Late November

I don't like it here. It's like being teased, when I stand on deck and look at all the people on shore. They're all so noisy. I don't mean bad noisy, I mean happy noisy. They're chatting and laughing with their friends and their children, and everything is so colourful and bright. When I think of London, everything seems so – well, sort of mud-coloured in my mind.

We have been given strange fruits to eat. Mrs Barnsley insists she's tried them all, but most of us have never been so lucky. The ones I know the names of are pineapples (nothing like apples), oranges and bananas, and there are several others whose names I can't remember. There is a huge basket of lemons and one of green limes on the deck, and we may help ourselves, but they are not fit for eating. Much too sour.

The 1st day of December

I cannot believe it can be so hot here yet in England it will be cold, and there will be snow and ice. My brothers and sisters will be huddling together in their beds for warmth, yet I cannot bear anyone to touch me because of the heat. The air sometimes feels thick and heavy. Sarah says John told her it's much worse on land. Everyone sleeps a lot when they can.

Mr Nicol has gone into the town to buy more fresh food for the journey. I think we must be leaving soon. I hope so.

Sarah was in his cabin most of the day, mending his clothes. She asked me to sit with her a while. I'm glad I did, because he has a box of tasty tidbits – sweetmeats and strange fruits that he's bought in Rio – and Sarah is allowed to help herself. She says her baby will come any day, she is sure.

I stitched a shirt sleeve for her, and she admired my work and asked where I learned to sew like that. I told her my mother had taught me, and she said I'm so good, she will let me do more sewing for Mr Nicol.

When we'd done enough, Sarah lolled on his bed and I sat in his chair, and we told each other stories, as we nibbled sweetmeats. When traders came aboard, the door was locked on us, so that they couldn't steal anything. We watched all the comings and goings through the tiny porthole.

'Don't you wish you could get into one of those little boats and sail away from the *Lady Juliana*?' I asked Sarah. She said she didn't, that she would be scared amongst all those crowds. I don't know if I do or if I don't. Certainly, the people of Rio seem very happy and jolly, and they don't eat people. It would be a good place to live. And maybe one day I would be able to sail all the way back to England.

Oh, stop dreaming, Mary Wade. If you did such a thing, you would be arrested and hanged.

The 2nd day of December

I am very stupid. I believed that Sarah would tell Mr Nicol that I had helped sew his clothes. But she didn't. When he saw her today, he kissed her and thanked her for taking such good care of his clothes and his cabin. She didn't mention me at all. She can do her own cuffs now.

The other stupid thing I did was tell Jane Whiting about the sweetmeats. She was livid because I didn't save her one. To be honest, it didn't even cross my mind, but I suppose I could have done. Still, there was no need for her to call me such horrible names. She really doesn't like me any more. Maybe she never did like me. Perhaps I was just someone to go round with in London, because she didn't have anyone her own age who liked her. I know she's never really forgiven me for going to collect her with the constable. But I really thought we'd end up close friends, because we're both in the same trouble, in the same boat, going to the same wild country.

We're on our way again. It is nearly the end of the year. How my life has changed since this time twelve months ago.

The 4th day of December

Sarah has had her baby. It's a beautiful little girl, and she has named her Viola. I asked her what sort of a name that was, and she said it was the name of a beautiful lady in a play she saw performed in the inn yard near her home. My ma had no love for fancy names. 'There's nothing wrong with being a plain Jane,' she would say. But I didn't say that to Sarah. She's a bit tearful, and I didn't want to upset her.

January 1790

I have made a decision. So many of the women on board fight and squabble all the time. Every time you turn round there are tears or quarrels or slaps or shouts. One woman has so annoyed everybody that hardly anyone has spoken to her for weeks. She grows more and more miserable and bad-tempered by the day. I started wondering what life will be like for her in New South Wales. That's if she's not murdered before she gets there. She is an outcast here. Imagine being an outcast when we land. With no one to care about her she will soon be killed and maybe even eaten.

I won't let that happen to me. I'm going to make sure I have friends in New South Wales. I am going to be kind and helpful to everybody. Well, to most people. There are some that I can't even bear to be near, like the woman who was sentenced for killing her own baby. How could anyone do such a thing? Rachel says we don't know the woman's true story, and her life might have been more awful than we think – so we shouldn't be too hard on her. I try to think kindly of the woman, but then I think of my own darling brothers and sisters and can't imagine how anyone could do such a thing.

But I need to get on with as many of the women as I can, especially the tough ones. If I do, I might be safe from being robbed or beaten up or even murdered. Also, if I was in trouble, it would mean I'd have friends to look after me. So, my plan is to look for things I can do for them, so they will owe me favours. And if I do something for someone, I'm going to make sure they know I've been helpful or whatever. I won't forget Sarah taking all the praise for my sewing.

End of January

Being kind and helpful is a good thing! Oh, I know it's what we're supposed to do if we want to go to heaven, but it's very useful down here on earth, too. People give you little rewards. Not all the women can do that, but quite a few have secret hoards of belongings, and some, like Mrs Barnsley, have money to buy little extras with. I'm getting to know who they are. I do odd jobs for Mrs Barnsley, like washing, or fetching and carrying things, or looking after things for her, particularly when she's off delivering a baby. We've got seven now. I like to help the mothers, especially Sarah, because I get a chance to cuddle the babies. It helps to make up for not being able to cuddle Hinny and the others. Well, helps a little.

Oh, this journey seems to be going on forever.

The 3rd day of February

A bad, bad day. I spent a couple of hours helping Sarah give Mr Nicol's cabin a good clean. I don't suppose he'll get to hear that I did it, but it was something to do. We left baby Viola sleeping on his bed while we worked. Then I looked for something else to occupy me.

Just after we left England, the captain gave Lieutenant Edgar some bales of linen, and told him to get some of the women busy making shirts to sell when we get to New South Wales. Most of them are useless at proper sewing. All they're able to do is mend a split seam or put a patch on their shifts. But some are really good with a needle and thread. I've sat with them a few times, watching, and sometimes, like today, if one of the women pricks her finger badly, I take over for a while until she stops bleeding. You don't want to get blood on a new shirt.

Today I was sitting chatting and enjoying the breeze, because it's really, really hot. Suddenly there was an almighty row coming from below.

'That sounds like Mrs Barnsley,' said Rachel. 'Nip down,

Mary, there's a love, and find out what the old sow's going on about.'

It turned out Mrs Barnsley had come back from delivering a really difficult baby. She'd washed all the muck off her hands, and gone back to the bundle of stuff she keeps hidden in the wool-work bag in her bedding. When she went to put her rings on, one of them was missing. She went berserk – that was the noise we heard – and sent her cronies to search for it.

'Turn over everyone's beds,' she was screeching. 'Everyone's!'

The cronies split up and went along every bed shelf, prodding and squeezing and poking. I hid behind a big wooden pillar and watched as they got near the shelf me and Jane sleep on. I was afraid they'd take my Bible, so I was ready to run up to them as if I'd just arrived, and say, 'That's mine. Give it back!'

But I never had a chance. Mean Moll patted my bed, felt the lumpy bit where my shoes and the Bible were wrapped in my shawl, and said, 'What's this?'

I ran towards her as she unwrapped it, then stopped in horror as she held something up and shouted, 'Lookee here, Lizzie Barnsley!'

It was a ring!

Before I knew it, Mrs Barnsley was in front of me, glaring. 'You sneaky little thief,' she said. 'You're stupid, you know

113

that? Did you think I wouldn't find it? What were you gonna do? Sell it to the natives for bananas and coconuts?'

I was shaking. But as I tried to tell her it wasn't me, I was conscious of Jane Whiting standing nearby, and she looked dead pleased with herself.

When Mrs Barnsley had worn herself out shouting, I managed to get a word in. 'How could I have taken it?' I said. 'I was with Sarah this morning, cleaning Mr Nicol's cabin, and then I stopped to help one of the shirtmakers. Ask them if you don't believe me!'

Someone bellowed for Sarah, and she came and told everyone I was speaking the truth. Then a couple of the shirtmakers said I'd been with them. I was so glad they backed me up. You can't tell with these women – sometimes they lie just for the sake of it.

Mrs Barnsley was silent for a moment, then she sent her cronies away and took me to a quiet corner. To my relief, she gave me back my Bible. Then she said, 'You'd better watch out, young 'un. Someone's gunning for you, and they're trying to get you into trouble.' She flicked my Bible with a finger. 'You'd better look after your book or you won't have it for long.'

I curled up in a ball on my bed and thought about what she said. I suspect Jane stole that ring and put it with my things. Why? Because she's jealous? What might she do next?

I took my Bible and went to find Sarah. She was walking on the deck with Mr Nicol. I'd planned to speak to her first, but as he was there I plucked up courage and said, 'Pardon me, sir. Could I ask you to do something special for me?'

He smiled. 'If it's something in my power, little Mary, you may certainly ask.'

'Please could you keep my Bible safe in your cabin, sir?' I asked. 'I'm frightened it might get stolen else.'

He smiled again. 'That I can do. Shall I take it from you now?'

I gave it to him.

'I know it's precious to you, little Mary,' he said. 'It will be safe with me.'

I thanked him, and I thought how Sarah looked down at me as if she was the lady of the manor. But at least she smiled, too.

The 5th day of February

We have been at sea more than four weeks since we left Rio, and there are as many more weeks to go before we reach our next port, maybe more. It is at a place called the Cape of Good Hope. It sounds nice. I hope it is.

Mid-February

The weather has been very hot and calm for days. We lie sweating on our beds at night. The sailors search the sky for clouds, and pray for a breath of wind.

A woman on the next sleeping shelf but one is very sick. Captain Aitken has given permission for her bed to be brought up on deck, so she can get what fresh air there is. I'm allowed to stay up there with her at night for a couple of hours, so I can give her water and wipe the sweat off her face. She's so weak. She doesn't speak.

It's nice on deck under the stars. Sometimes, if I'm very

quiet, they forget to send me back down below, and I stay there all night.

The 14th of February, St Valentine's Day

A seaman woke me this morning. The woman I've been staying on deck with died in the night. She must have just gone in her sleep, for I heard nothing. The day feels chilly and I was glad to go below. A storm is brewing.

John Nicol gave Sarah a poem in honour of St Valentine, she said. She has tucked it inside her bodice, and keeps patting it. She doesn't know what it says, for I know she cannot read. So does John Nicol, I'm sure. He could have given her his shopping list for all she'd know.

Later

The most horrible thing has happened. I can't even think about it without crying most terribly.

117

The 15th day of February

I'm calmer today, though tears still escape from my eyes and I can't stop them.

The dead woman can't be buried, of course, because it will be a while before we reach land. They said she would be buried at sea, and I felt sick with horror at the thought of being left all alone, in the deep, deep water, and never being found again.

With the weather so bad, I thought they'd put the burial off, but they didn't. Everyone was on deck, and the woman's body was in a rough coffin of thin wood, that the carpenter had made. We had to hold on to whatever we could, because the ship was rolling quite badly, and it was hard to keep our feet.

The captain came to do the prayers, and even he found it hard to walk straight. Then he said a few words to one of his officers, who said to John Nicol, 'Captain's not bringing the ship's good Bible out in this weather – the rain will ruin it. He wants you to fetch another.'

The crew sang a hymn and the women who knew the words joined in. I didn't. Soon Mr Nicol returned.

I gasped with surprise. The Bible was black. The size of a man's hand. It had gold lettering. It was mine!

In a way, I felt it was nice that my Bible was to be used to send this poor woman to her rest. I felt quite proud.

The captain took it from Mr Nicol, and I couldn't see what happened next, as there were some big women and a group of seamen in front of me. I was concentrating hard on keeping my balance and holding on to the rail. But I heard him reading, though I couldn't catch the words because the wind was howling and someone behind me was being sick.

Suddenly, the ship lurched horribly and I was thrown against the side. To my horror, I saw the captain fall and grab the ship's rail.

He dropped my Bible! It fell into the sea and was swallowed up. I cried out, but the women were yelling and some were screaming, and my words were whipped away by the wind. The coffin was hastily tipped overboard, and everyone scurried for shelter.

I stayed for a moment, staring at the black water, but a seaman took my arm and flung me down below. 'It ain't safe up here,' he cried.

I threw myself on my bed, and buried my face in my arms. I was upset. I was angry. I cried. I slept.

By the time the storm was over, I'd remembered something Ma always said. 'It's no use crying over spilt milk.' And she used to say, 'Least said, soonest mended.' And

'What's done is done, and that's all there is to it.'

It comforted me a little that Ma's words came into my mind just then, when I was upset and angry about her Bible.

So, that's it. My Bible's gone. No use crying. I must forget it. I will try hard not to think of it again.

Four days later

Sarah Whitlam is cross with me, I know, because I have been in a huddle all by myself for a few days. I haven't wanted to speak to anyone, not even baby Viola, and I definitely don't want to speak to Sarah or Mr Nicol. He could have sent a message to me about my Bible. He could have said sorry. But he didn't. I suppose a thing like a book is nothing to a man with fine clothes and lots of books to read and books to write in.

Mrs Barnsley got hold of me and told me to stop feeling sorry for myself, and come and help make baby clothes, so that's what I've been doing. I don't want to get her crabby with me. And it's been nice in a way, because as I stitch I have a little daydream. I imagine I have a baby of my own, a boy, and I'm expecting another. That's why I'm making baby clothes. And I'm waiting for my husband to come home, and there's a fine stew, with onions, bubbling away on our own fire. And I'm happy.

Five days later

I hardly ever know what the date is these days, because I haven't been near Mr Nicol's cabin. Sarah can get someone else to clean it. It's days since I've even looked at either of them, but today I had to. Lieutenant Edgar found me on deck, staring over the rail at the sea as it rushed past.

'Take this to Mr Nicol's cabin,' he said. 'You know where it is.' And he handed me a book. 'Please thank him kindly for the loan of it,' he added.

I took my time. I really wanted to fling the book overboard, but I sensed that the lieutenant was watching me, so I dragged my heels.

I knocked on the door.

'Come,' said Mr Nicol.

He was hunched up, reading by the light of his lantern. Reading his own Bible. It made me angry, but I kept my temper and held out the book. 'Lieutenant Edgar says thank you kindly for the loan of it,' I said, without looking him in the eye. Then I left. As I shut the door, I heard him call, 'Mary? Mary Wade!' But I ran and hid. I don't want to hear his slimy words. If he was truly sorry about my Bible, he would have said so at the time. It's just another book to him.

The 1st day of March

We are at the place called the Cape of Good Hope in a bay called Table Bay. From the ship I can see the strangest mountain. On our travels, I have seen mountains, but never one like this. It is completely flat on top, as if some giant has taken a great sword and sliced the peak away. It's called Table Mountain. This morning it looks stranger than ever. There is a long flat cloud sitting on top of it, and wisps of cloud are drifting over the edge and down the sides. It looks just as if a giant has laid a snowy cloth on his table, ready for dinner.

We have been here for days, and the crew are all of a fidget. We expected to meet the *Guardian*, the ship full of supplies, but she isn't here.

The weather is sunny, but quite cold. I'm glad the sun is not burning hot any more. I've had enough of it. Rachel says that my hair is much fairer now than it was when she first met me.

'It's the sun that does it,' she said. 'It makes our faces dark, and our hair light!'

She's quite right, but I don't see how that can be.

The 3rd day of March

Now we know why the crew have been fidgety, and Captain Aitken has looked so worried. The *Guardian* isn't here because it crashed into an island. Not an ordinary island, but one made entirely of ice! There are many of these, it seems, floating around the oceans. I hope we do not meet one. though it would be interesting to see. The largest piece of ice I ever saw at home was an icicle the length of a grown man. Ma said if it fell on me it would pierce my head, but I'm quite sure it couldn't damage a huge ship.

How terrible it must have been to crash and feel your ship break beneath you.

Many of the *Guardian*'s crew disappeared. Nobody knows if they drowned, or if they escaped in small boats. I should hate to be on the wide open sea in a tiny rowing boat. The captain and a few others stayed on the wreck, and were eventually brought to the Cape of Good Hope by a ship from the Americas. They were lucky.

But we are not lucky. Because of the shipwreck, we are to sail into Port Jackson, in New South Wales, without all the supplies that the *Guardian* was to have brought for us. So our captain is loading the *Lady Juliana* with as much as she can carry.

The 5th day of March

Today everyone had to stay below, while the ship was being loaded with fresh cargo. We couldn't make out what it was. There were the strangest noises. When we were finally allowed up, we saw what it was. A great flock of sheep, and a very noisy, angry ram!

Lieutenant Edgar asked who among us is used to tending sheep. Four women put their hands up, and so did I. I thought it would be fun to look after animals.

He looked at me sternly. 'You are a little young to have been a shepherdess.'

I told him my pa was a drover, which was true, and that I often helped him with his work, which was a lie. In the end he chose a woman we call Woolly Moll, because she has a matted old sheepskin which she never leaves anywhere. I think he picked her because she looks the strongest. She was thrilled to have sheep to look after, and immediately went to make friends with them.

Lieutenant Edgar called me to him. 'You may help the

shepherdess if you wish,' he said. 'She is to be in charge of the sheep on our voyage, and she must keep them healthy.'

I said I will help her when I can, but I probably won't, because I don't like Woolly Moll much.

Mid-March

Fire!

I was never so afraid for my life. Well, apart from when I was sentenced to death, of course.

The ship's carpenter often has a stinking pot of pitch boiling away, with a fire beneath it. He uses the melted pitch to make the joins between planks waterproof. You cannot float a boat, he says, if water seeps between the planks. Everyone on board ship is careful about fire, because if a ship burns, there is nothing to carry the people away from it. You'd think we would have been safe from fire, with the whole of the ocean around us, but no. The pitch boiled over and spread across the deck, and the flames leapt along it and high into the air!

Everyone screamed; all the women, that is. The animals in their pens on deck stamped and kicked and bellowed and clucked pitifully as smoke billowed all around. Mr Nicol himself was a hero. He fetched blankets and did his best to keep the flames down until help arrived with buckets and buckets of water. The men made themselves into a chain, passing buckets from hand to hand until all was safe and the deck was thoroughly soaked.

Afterwards, I saw the captain shake Mr Nicol's hand, and heard him praising him for his quick actions. 'You will be rewarded,' he told him.

I suppose I am grateful that Mr Nicol saved the ship from burning, but I despise him. I know it is not his fault that the Bible went overboard, but he might have said something to me about it. But then, I suppose, I am nothing to him.

End of March

We are all experienced sailors now, and can tell by the mad activity of the seamen that we are leaving Cape Town soon. Everyone has to keep out of their way, so that means being cooped up in the hold.

Mrs Barnsley was sick right in front of me today.

The 2nd of April

Now we have left the Cape of Good Hope, I keep thinking that our next port will be Port Jackson, our final one. But it won't be for several more weeks, so I must try to put it out of my mind.

There's such a fuss down in our sleeping hold. Mrs Barnsley woke up really poorly this morning. I didn't go near her, in case I catch whatever she's got, but all the time, there's her little group of cronies crowded round her. Each woman is trying to be the one to please her the most, and get in her good books. They all think she's going to be so generous with her possessions when we reach New South Wales, but I bet she keeps everything to herself. I would.

I went up on deck as soon as we were allowed out, and sat with the sewing women. They talk a lot about what will happen when we get to Port Jackson. Most of us are scared, but one woman, called Jenny, said we're all stupid, because we're not scared of something real, we're scared of the unknown.

'Time enough to be scared when we get there,' she said. 'It's a waste of time being scared now. Just enjoy the sunshine and the fresh air. And the good food.'

'But what about the wild animals?' another woman said scornfully. 'Are you telling me you ain't scared about them?'

Jenny looked around. 'Can't see any lions or tigers or bears right now,' she said. 'So no, I ain't scared of them.'

'I'm scared of being killed with a spear and being boiled alive in a big cooking pot,' I said.

Jenny laughed. 'You'll never be boiled for anyone's dinner,' she said. 'There ain't enough meat on you for a bowl of pottage.'

That set everyone off into fits of giggles, even me.

Mid-April

The sea was a bit rough this morning, so we were kept below for safety. A lot of people get ill when the ship rolls and tosses, and the whole of our sleeping deck smells of sick. Mrs Barnsley is very quiet. All you can hear from her corner is the cronies, squabbling. The latest arguments are all about who keeps swiping her food, and every now and then there's a squeal, as if someone's been pinched hard, and then a voice hissing, 'I didn't steal nothing! It was someone else. Her! It was her!' Then whoever 'her' is starts up all over again.

I hate the days when we're kept below. One of the men who sends our food down said we ought to stop grumbling and give thanks that we're not slaves. They get left below in chains, crammed together, with just bread and water to keep them alive. Or ship's biscuits, which are horrible and have creatures in them.

Late April

All the days seem the same at the moment. The only thing we see is water, and sometimes clouds. Birds, too, now and then. Yesterday, a big white bird followed the *Lady Juliana* for ages. I thought of B'nore, the great white bird in Hinny's favourite story. For a moment, just a moment, I felt as if she was close to me.

Sometimes there are ships, and we stop, so Captain Aitken can be rowed across to chat to the other captains. I don't mind it when we stop. Although I would love to be ashore again, I'm afraid of what we might have to face in the new land, so the longer it takes to get there, the better.

I spilt water on my spare shift this morning, so I dried it up on deck, then took it back down to leave tucked in my bed. It hasn't been stolen because it's too small for anyone else. While I was down there I heard whispering coming from Mrs Barnsley's corner.

I crept nearer, and hid behind a wooden pillar to listen. The cronies were making a plan to take turns looking after her, just two of them at a time.

'But suppose she wakes up and sees it's just you two?' said one. 'You'd be the ones to get any handouts, wouldn't you? And the rest of us would get nothing.'

'Shut up, Peg!' snapped Mean Moll. 'She might hear you.'

'Oh, she's not hearing anything,' said Nelly Rednose. 'Look at the state of her. She's too ill to know whether it's day or night. Now what about it? How are we going to make this fair?'

I didn't dare move in case they heard me.

There was a lot of whispered squabbling, then Nelly Rednose's voice, louder than the others, said, 'It's easy. We just make an agreement and we swear on it.'

There was a moment of silence. All I could hear was Mrs Barnsley's fast, harsh breathing.

'Anything one of us gets,' said Peg, 'we share, right? Moll? Dolly? Nelly?'

They all agreed, then Peg made them all swear on their lives that the six of them would share anything Mrs Barnsley gave them for taking care of her. 'Speaking of which,' she said, 'someone had better get her something to drink.'

They argued so loudly about who would fetch the water

that I was able to slip away, just as they decided it should be Softheaded Dolly.

What a rotten lot they are. They suck up to Mrs Barnsley, just so they can get whatever she's kind enough to give them. And they're not even looking after her properly. I know I haven't always got on with her, but I'm sure I wouldn't stand arguing over her while she got worse and worse. At least I'd see she got some water and food.

I was glad to get up on deck. Some of the women were singing and dancing down at the back of the ship, and it was fun to watch them. It set the chickens off clucking like mad, which made me laugh.

It can't be long till we reach New South Wales. I looked round at everyone and wondered how much time we all have to live. I thought about the poor woman who died. She didn't even get a chance to face the wild animals and snakes and deadly spiders and things.

End of April

The surgeon, Mr Alley, said that Mrs Barnsley shouldn't be down below in that dreadful heat. He had her carried up on deck, with her belongings in her red-and-blue wool-work bag. They laid out bedding for her in a corner behind the bull's pen. Mr Nicol and he had a talk and then Mr Alley looked round and beckoned to me.

My stomach got in a knot, even though I knew I hadn't done anything wrong. But I needn't have worried. All he said was, 'Mary Wade, it is to be your job to stay with Mrs Barnsley and watch her, day and night. If there are any changes, you must send for me. You may ask any seaman who is idle to fetch me.'

I nodded to him. I didn't even look at Mr Nicol.

'And I want you to try to give her a little water whenever possible, and some broth, if you can. Your own meals will be sent to you.'

He turned to Mr Nicol and said, 'It's all we can do. She is very, very ill.' And he shook his head.

As they strolled away, I was suddenly surrounded by all Mrs Barnsley's cronies. Their angry faces were so close I could see little red lines in their eyes.

'Why you?' said Mean Moll.

'How come you can look after her and we can't?' said Nelly Rednose.

Mr Nicol stopped and turned. 'Ladies, be calm,' he said. 'Mr Alley and I chose Mary to watch over Mrs Barnsley because she is so young that she is unlikely to try to escape at night.'

'Escape?' said Nelly. 'How could anyone escape? We're in the middle of the flaming sea!'

Softheaded Dolly said, 'We could take one of the little rowing boats.'

'Exactly,' said Mr Nicol. 'Mary is unlikely to attempt that, I think you'll agree. Also,' he added, 'she is unlikely to murder any of us in our beds. Now go about your business.'

He turned and winked at me. I was furious at being caught looking at him, and looked away.

The women glared at me, and there was a great deal of head-tossing and humphing as they sauntered off.

My bedding has been brought to me by a seaman. I checked that my things were still there and spread it out beside Mrs Barnsley. If the wind stays in the right direction the stench from the bull's pen will not bother me much.

Without doubt, looking after Mrs Barnsley is the most boring thing I've ever done. She does nothing, says nothing, just lies as if asleep. But how lovely to be in the fresh air, all the time, with my food and drink brought to me. I feel like a real lady!

The beginning of May

Mrs Barnsley seems weaker. I get a little water between her lips whenever I can, but that's all. It doesn't seem to be making her better. When I look at her, lying in the shade, I think of my ma. She looked just the same when she was so ill after having baby Jem. I sat by her side then, dripping little droplets of broth between her lips, to try to make her well and strong. Thinking about that made me cry, but no one could see my tears.

Elizabeth Barnsley's cronies watch and wait. They're sure she's dying. I'm just annoyed that while I'm here, I can't be doing good turns for people who might help me when we land.

The 3rd day of May

I sent for the surgeon this morning. Mrs Barnsley's breathing is weaker. He shook his head, and told me to stay with her. 'Not long now,' he said.

I'm not going to let her die.

Later

When my dinner came, I got my spoon and put a tiny amount of the thin gravy from the stew into Mrs Barnsley's mouth. I was a bit worried she might choke, but it was only a few drops, and she's going to die anyway.

She didn't choke. I kept my bowl with me all afternoon, and gave her a drop of gravy every once in a while. Again, she didn't choke, and she wasn't sick.

When the surgeon came to see her at dusk, he bent down and felt her wrist and her forehead, and held his lantern over her face. 'Hmm,' was all he said.

'I've been giving her a little gravy, Mr Alley,' I told him. I thought it best to say the truth.

He looked surprised. 'And did she take it?'

'Well, she didn't seem to know she was having it, sir,' I said. 'I just shoved it in her mouth.'

He looked at my bowl and said, 'I'll get something more nourishing.' He patted my head. 'For both of you.'

I curled up, leaning against a chest. When I heard footsteps, I saw it was Mr Nicol, so I closed my eyes and pretended to be asleep. He must have stood looking at Mrs Barnsley for a moment or two, but then I felt my cover being laid over me.

That was quite nice of him, but it doesn't make me forgive him for getting my Bible lost and never saying sorry.

The 4th day of May

The food Mr Alley sends is a rich broth, thick with barley. There are always two bowls, and I empty mine in no time. It's the tastiest food I've had since I left home. If anything's going to do Mrs Barnsley good, this is it. I spoon the tiniest amount into her mouth, but much more often than yesterday.

In the middle of the day, when it was too hot for anyone

to do anything, the cronies appeared, wandering casually up to where I sat beside Mrs Barnsley.

'We came to see how our dear friend is,' said Nelly Rednose. Softheaded Dolly and enormous Peg knelt down, blocking my view. Mean Moll went round the other side. They were so quiet I suspected they were up to no good, so I poked my head between the two nearest backsides.

Suddenly, a rough hand pushed me so hard in the face that I fell backwards, but not before I saw what was going on. One of them was rooting about inside Mrs Barnsley's bed, and the other was fishing in her wool-work bag.

There was a cry of rage from Mean Moll.

'What! Nothing?' said Peg.

'A used kerchief, her tablet of soap and her best petticoat,' snapped Mean Moll. 'We'll have those.' Then she turned her angry face towards me. 'Don't you look at me like that, Miss Mealymouth Mary. She won't need this where she's going.'

I wasn't scared. I was angry. 'She's not going anywhere,' I shouted, 'because I won't let her!'

'Oho!' sneered Peg. 'We know what you're up to, sucking up to her, so you can get her possessions. Well, we're watching you, miss.'

'You needn't bother,' I said. 'She hasn't got anything. You've proved that yourselves.'

Thank goodness, Mr Alley arrived just then. The cronies slyly patted my cheek as they left, saying things like, 'What a little angel,' and 'Bless the child.'

Mr Alley smiled as he watched them go. 'They must be missing their friend.' He knelt down to look at Mrs Barnsley. 'Hmm,' he said. Then again, 'Hmm. Are you still feeding her, Mary?'

'As much as I can,' I said.

He smiled. 'By the look of Mrs Barnsley's colour, you might be doing her some good.'

The 6th day of May

Mr Alley has continued to send what he calls 'nourishment', for both of us. It's wonderful to have food with so much flavour. There was a fish soup this morning, with things floating in it. At home I would have refused it, and made do with bread, but I've learnt not to be so fussy. Anyway, I closed my eyes when I ate it, and it tasted delicious.

Even I can see the difference in Mrs Barnsley. Her lips are pinker. All our faces have been cooked brown in the sun, but lately she has looked deathly pale. Today, though, there's a slight blush on her cheeks.

I do believe she's going to get better.

The 8th day of May

What a terrible fright I had this morning! I had washed the sweat off Mrs Barnsley's face as usual, and run my fingers through her hair. Then I tidied her bed and made sure she was shaded by the awning the seamen put up for her.

As I reached to pat her pillow, her hand shot up and grabbed my wrist so tightly I cried out. My heart pounded. For a moment I thought she had died and this was what Ma once described as the last twitches.

Her voice was so hoarse I could barely make out her words.

'What are you doing, Mary Wade?' Then she knocked me aside and tried to sit up.

'No,' I cried, 'you mustn't...'

Suddenly, I was on the deck in a flurry of other people's skirts, as the cronies rushed across to her.

'Lizzie, darling, you've come back to us!'

'We've waited and prayed for you!'

'Saints be praised, you're well again!'

What a lot of pig swill. They don't care about Mrs Barnsley. They only care for what they can get out of her.

I went to find Mr Alley. He told me to wait for him. I sat in his cabin and tried to read his journal, but his writing is terrible.

When he came back, he said I'd done a fine job, and he believes Mrs Barnsley will recover fully. As our journey's nearly over, he's going to let her sleep in a little hut-thing on deck. There's only just room for her in there, so she'll be on her own. I suppose he thinks she hasn't got the strength to escape.

It was horrible having to move back to the orlop hold after being in the fresh air all the time. I liked the cool air at night. Down here it's sweltering, and it smells of dirty bodies and dead rats and poo.

The 10th day of May

Elizabeth Barnsley sent for me this afternoon. I went to her hut. She was sitting outside and had her old colour back again.

I didn't say anything, because I didn't know what to say. I just stood there.

'Come nearer,' she said.

I moved closer, and she reached up, grabbed my hand and

pulled me down beside her.

'Mr Nicol's been talking to me about you.'

'Oh,' I said, thinking, I bet he never mentioned my Bible.

'He told me it was you what nursed me, and Mr Alley said you did a fine job.'

I nodded.

She went on. 'He said you nursed me when everyone else had given me up for dead.'

I nodded again. Then I said, 'I'm sorry all your belongings have gone. I saw some people take your petticoat and your soap and your kerchief, but all the rest – your money and jewellery – they must have been taken before I started looking after you. I never touched anything, honest.'

She smiled. 'I know you didn't, Mary Wade. Months ago, I asked Lieutenant Edgar to look after my belongings.' She gave a hoarse laugh, then coughed. 'All these criminals on board, I knew I didn't have a chance of keeping them safe till we get to Port Jackson. Any time I needed anything, I asked him.'

'That was clever,' I said, wishing I'd given my Bible to Lieutenant Edgar instead of John Nicol. How could I ever have thought him so very kind?

Mrs Barnsley patted my hand. 'I won't forget what you did for me, Mary Wade.'

I hope she remembers that next time she's annoyed with me.

Mid-May

I've been getting on all right with Mrs Barnsley. It'll be a day or two before she's strong enough to look after herself, so I've been seeing she gets her food and everything. She's told me a bit about herself. I was surprised to hear that she's got children at home in England.

'Fair broke my heart to leave them,' she said, 'but I'll see them again one day.'

'My ma won't ever see me again,' I said.

The end of May

Everyone is fidgety and anxious, and there are more fights and quarrels than ever. I think it's because we're getting near Port Jackson, and everyone's scared of what it'll be like. I wish I had a friend, a true friend, so we could look out for each other. Jane and I hardly speak since that ring business and, besides, she's worse than useless. Sarah's too wrapped up with baby Viola, and she's got Mr Nicol, anyway. She doesn't need me.

There's endless talk about what we might expect. Lieutenant Edgar has given little speeches about it, and told us there aren't any lions or tigers. He said the giant hopping animals are called kangaroos, and they have pockets to keep their babies in. I couldn't stop laughing at that! And, he said, the pretty bear creatures in the trees are called koalas.

'If you leave them alone,' he said, 'these creatures won't harm you.'

'What about the snakes and spiders?' someone called.

He looked a bit uncomfortable. 'I'm sure they won't bother you.'

Mean Moll laughed. 'If I see a spider, it won't bother me, because it'll be dead before it gets a chance to!'

One thing we do know is that we've had it easy the last few months. We're going to have to work really hard. I'm good at working hard, but I won't know what to do. I told Mrs Barnsley I'm afraid because I don't know how to grow crops or build huts or milk cows, and I'm sure she doesn't, either.

She laughed. 'The trick is, ducks,' she said, 'to get other people to do it for you.'

I never thought of that.

The day we reached Port Jackson

We have arrived at New South Wales and by this afternoon we will be stepping off the ship on to our new land. That is disturbing and exciting enough, but the most surprising thing has already happened. We were sailing along the coast, and I was leaning on the rail with Mrs Barnsley, trying to see what it's like, when a voice behind me said, 'Here you are, Mary.'

I turned. It was Mr Nicol.

'This is yours,' he said. 'It's time for you to take it back.'

I looked down at what he was holding, and my heart seemed to leap into my mouth. I reached out.

It was my Bible.

'But... b-but...' I stammered.

He frowned. 'You seem astonished. I know there's a little white mould on the cover – that can't be helped in hot climates...'

I looked up at him. My eyes were teary and blurred. 'But I thought... The captain lost my Bible overboard in the storm. I saw it.'

He frowned even more, then the lines across his forehead

smoothed out. 'Oh that. No, that was my Bible – the one I always kept on board ship.'

I didn't understand. 'But I saw you reading yours after that, in your cabin.'

'No, no,' he said. 'Captain Aitken gave me that one to replace the one he lost overboard. We're carrying a whole stock of Bibles to give to the people in Port Jackson.' He put my own Bible firmly into my hands. 'Here, take it. It's yours.'

I clutched it to my chest and burst into tears. As Mr Nicol walked away, Mrs Barnsley put an arm around my shoulders.

'There, there, ducks. What's all the crying about? You've got your book, though what you want it for, I'm sure I don't know.'

'My ma's. It was my ma's,' I blubbed, and I found myself gabbling out the story of the Bible, and how desperately I wanted Ma to have it back. 'And now she never will,' I wailed, 'and I've got to go ashore and I've got no family and I'm all alone in the world...'

She hugged me. 'You stick with me, ducks,' she said quietly. 'I ain't been much of a mother, Lord knows, but I'll do me best for you. Look!' She pointed to the coast. 'It don't look so bad. There's trees and stuff, and I can't see any pots of water being boiled up, so they ain't planning to eat us straight away.'

At this, I wailed even louder, but she laughed and hugged

me again. 'Only joking, ducks. You'll be safe with me, I promise. I owe you my life. I ain't going to let anyone mess yours up, am I?'

I relaxed, then, with my head leaning against her shoulder. I have someone who has promised to be like a mother to me.

I stroked the mouldy cover of my Bible. It is a little piece of my own mother, and it will help me never to forget her. Inside are the names of all my brothers and sisters, so I will never forget them, even if they forget me.

If I live, I will do my best to be happy in this new land. I will.

And afterwards...

A year after Mary Wade was sentenced to death, she began a new life on the other side of the world.

When the *Lady Juliana* reached New South Wales, the passengers and crew were greeted with dismay by those in charge. The first colonists were desperate for supplies, and were appalled to learn of the loss of the *Guardian*. It would be impossible to feed all the new arrivals, so a number of them, including Mary, were sent to beautiful Norfolk Island, to the east of Australia, where another colony had been set up a year or so earlier.

Over the next few years, Mary and her partner, a man called Teague Harrigan, had two children. By the year 1800 they had moved to Sydney, and Mary had given birth to a third child. The relationship broke up when Teague left her to join a ship on a whaling expedition.

Within a short while, Mary was living with her new partner, a furniture maker called Jonathan Brooker. Once they were freed from their sentences, they began farming successfully on 30 acres of land near Sydney. It was a hard life, and it must have been the bitterest blow when everything they owned was destroyed in a bush fire.

Both Mary and Jonathan were made of strong stuff, and it wasn't many years before they rebuilt their lives on a new 62 acre farm. Over the years they had eighteen more children, and lived together until Jonathan's death in 1833.

Mary lived a further 26 years, and died in 1859 aged 80, leaving a huge number of children, grandchildren and great-grandchildren. She was buried in a churchyard at a place called Fairy Meadow, and it must have been a source of pride to her that the land the church was built on was donated by one of her own sons.

Thousands of modern-day Australians, including a former prime minister, are descended from the one-time child thief, and are proud that their ancestor, Mary Wade, is known as one of the founding mothers of Australia.

Experience history first-hand with My Story –
a series of vividly imagined accounts of life in the past.

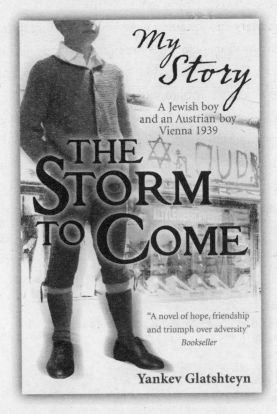

My Story

A Jewish boy
and an Austrian boy
Vienna 1939

THE
STORM
TO COME

"A novel of hope, friendship
and triumph over adversity"
Bookseller

Yankev Glatshteyn

Emil and Karl are best friends. Emil is a Jew;
Karl isn't. When three men take Karl's
mother away, who knows where, and the Nazis
murder Emil's father, the two boys find
themselves alone and scared, wandering in an
increasingly hostile city. Who can they trust
and where can they go...?

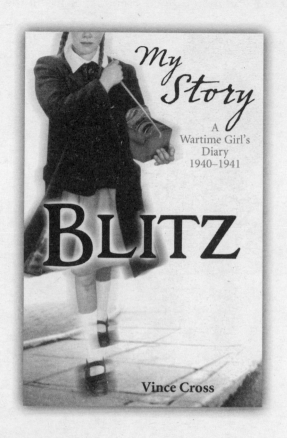

My Story

A Wartime Girl's Diary 1940–1941

BLITZ

Vince Cross

It's 1940 and with London under fire Edie and her little brother are evacuated to Wales. Miles from home and missing her family, Edie is determined to be strong, but when life in the countryside proves tougher than in the capital she is torn between obeying her parents and protecting her brother...

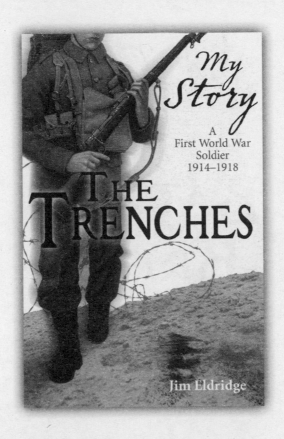

My
Story

A
First World War
Soldier
1914–1918

THE
TRENCHES

Jim Eldridge

It's 1917 and Billy Stevens is a telegraph
operator stationed near Ypres. The Great War
has been raging for three years when Billy finds
himself taking part in the deadly Big Push forward.
But he is shocked to discover that the bullets
of his fellow soldiers aren't just
aimed at the enemy...

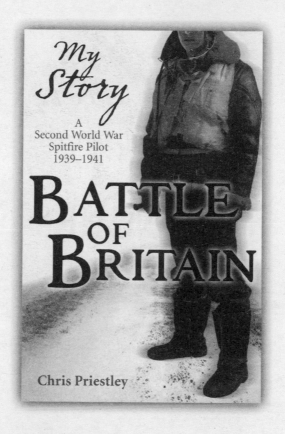

My Story

A
Second World War
Spitfire Pilot
1939–1941

BATTLE
OF
BRITAIN

Chris Priestley

It's 1939 and Harry Woods is a
Spitfire pilot in the RAF. When his friend
Lenny loses his leg in a dogfight with the
Luftwaffe, Harry is determined to fight on.
That is, until his plane is hit and he finds
himself tumbling through the air
high above the English Channel...

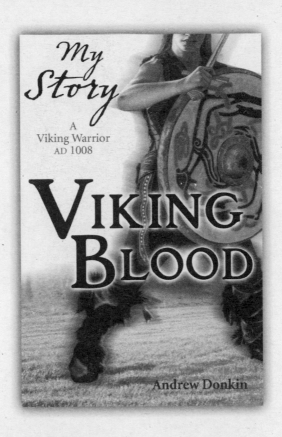

It's AD 1008, and after being injured in a raid
that goes horribly wrong, Tor Scaldbane
is devastated at losing his chance to be a
legendary warrior.

But then he discovers the sagas of his ancestors; glorious,
bloody battles, ancient heroes, powerful gods ... and
realizes that all might not be lost after all...

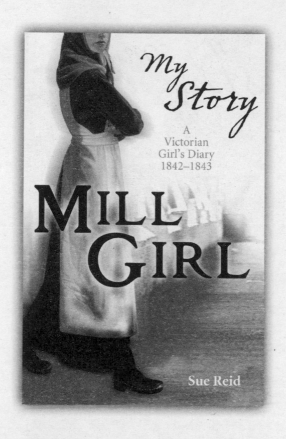

My Story

A
Victorian
Girl's Diary
1842–1843

MILL
GIRL

Sue Reid

In spring 1842 Eliza is shocked when
she is sent to work in the Manchester cotton
mills – the noisy, suffocating mills. The work is
backbreaking and dangerous – and when she sees her
friends' lives wrecked by poverty, sickness
and unrest, Eliza realizes she must fight to escape
the fate of a mill girl...

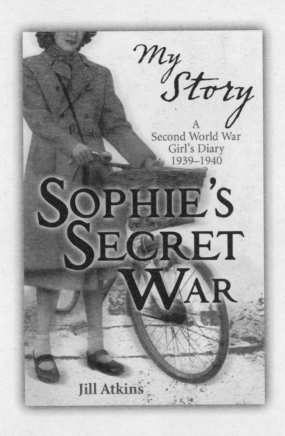

My Story

A Second World War Girl's Diary 1939–1940

SOPHIE'S SECRET WAR

Jill Atkins

In 1939, the start of the Second World War, Sophie becomes a messenger for a Resistance group in Northern France. But as the German invaders overwhelm the British forces on the French coast, Sophie finds herself more deeply involved with the Resistance – in a dangerous plan to save a young Scottish soldier...

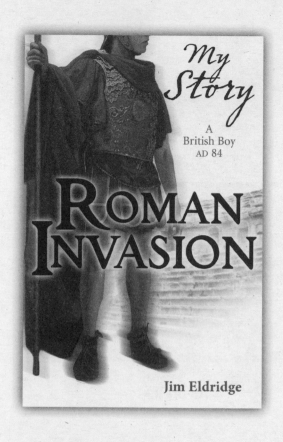

My
Story

A
British Boy
AD 84

ROMAN
INVASION

Jim Eldridge

It's AD 84 when Bran, a prince of the
Carvetii tribe, is captured by the Romans.
A legion of soldiers is marching east, to
build a military road. It's hostile
country, and Bran is to go with them as a
hostage to ensure the legion's safety ... but
no one is safe in newly conquered Britain.